One Tough Cookie

A Carol Sabala Mystery

Vinnie Hansen

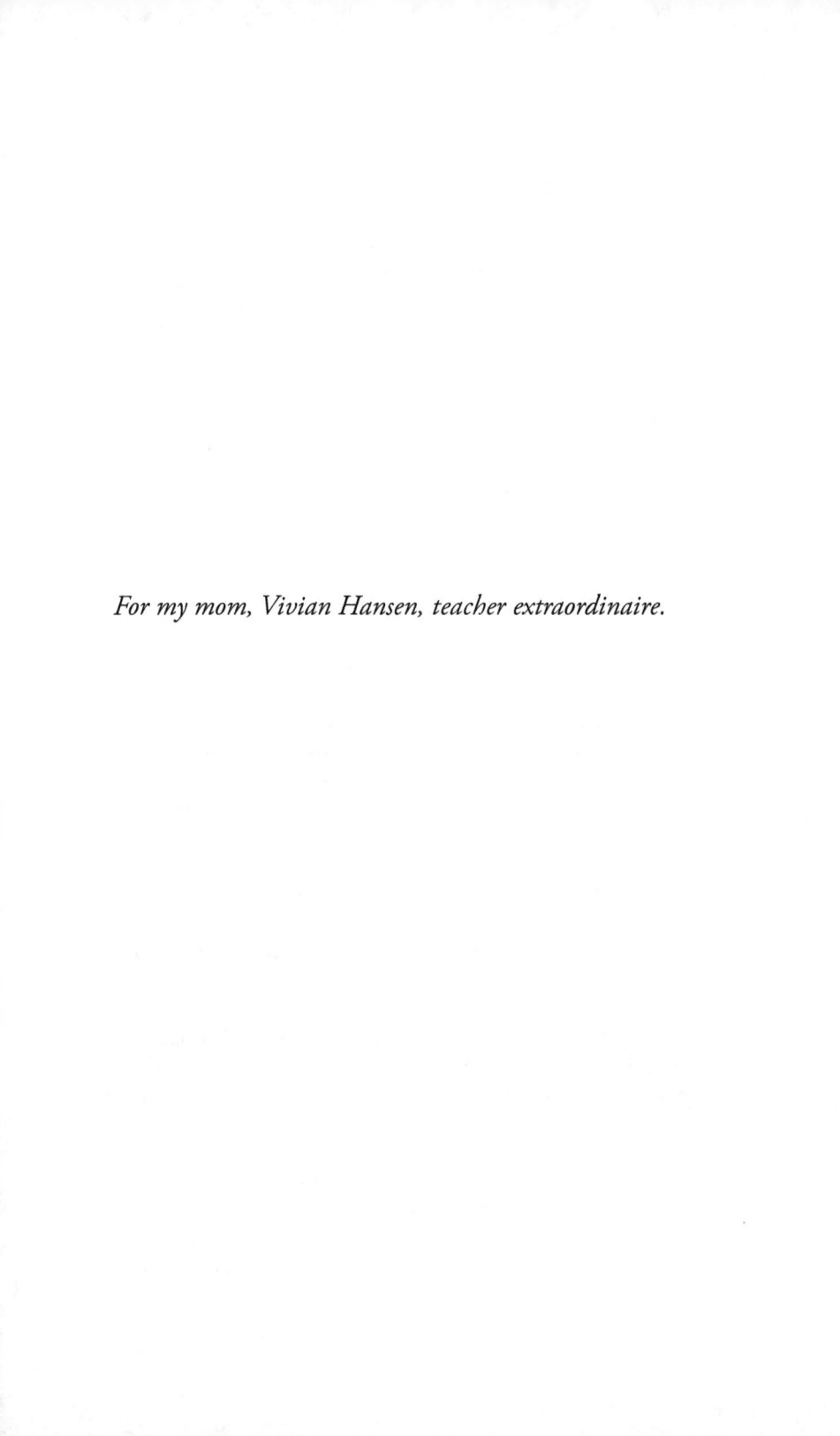

For my mom, Vivian Hansen, teacher extraordinaire.

PRAISE FOR HANSEN'S WORK

"With edgy precision, Hansen applies all the elements of a good mystery: interesting plot, compelling characters, a finely drawn sense of place, and excellent writing. One Tough Cookie *has made me a fan, one who can't wait to gorge on* Rotten Dates.*"*
--Denise Osborne, author of *Feng Shui Mysteries*
and Queenie Davilov Mysteries

Black Beans & Venom – Claymore Award Finalist.

"Her writing style is like liquid poetry. Her characters rule the page, and the action moves smoothly from one scene to the next."
Midwest Book Review

"I love Carol Sabala...quirky, gutsy and my kind of gal in an aqua tank top."
--Cara Black, Author of the Aimée Leduc mystery series

"Hansen's sense of humor and protagonist make for a good read. I particularly enjoyed her faithfully rendered Santa Cruz background."
--Laura Crum, author of the Gail McCarthy murder mystery series

"The pacing of Hansen's story is excellent."
--Chris Watson, *Santa Cruz Sentinel* on *Murder, Honey*

"I just finished Murder, Honey *and I found it splendid."*
--Laura Davis, author of *Courage to Heal*

"In Sabala, Hansen has created a likable sleuth whose many problems readers may readily identify with, and as far as Carol's mother goes—well, let's just say I hope we see more of her in the future."
--Michael Cornelius, *The Bloomsbury Review*

"Five silver pens out of five for 'Tang Is Not Juice.'*"*
--Silas Spaeth, *Salinas Californian*

"Best Book of Fiction of 2005" for Tang Is Not Juice
Oklahoma Writers' Federation, Inc.

1994

CHAPTER 1

Thirty teenagers stared at me. They were neither rude nor terribly interested. Alvina Jameson, the teacher, had herded the students into two concentric semicircles before the stainless steel table. I wanted to shoo them back a full step. I could hear one kid's wheezy breathing.

"I thought she'd be a man," a tall boy in the outer circle whispered.

A tiny girl with long, long hair whipped around. "Geez, Chendo, Mrs. Jameson told us her name was Carol Sabala."

Despite the boy's assumption about a baker, society had cut inroads into sexism. About one third of the cooking class was male. A few of the students appeared mildly curious about what I would concoct with the flour, yeast, eggs, almond extract, and sugar. I was a little curious, too. I'd made Danish dough hundreds of times, but never in such a small quantity, and never for an audience. Of course, it didn't matter if the recipe flopped, as I'd lugged in a five-gallon bucket of chilled, prepared dough for the actual baking.

The group hovered with limited jockeying, and my admiration soared for Alvina Jameson, who smiled encouragingly at me from the end of the table. I rolled up the sleeves of my chef's jacket, and pushed up the cuffs of the pink turtleneck under it.

"First you need flour. . . ."

A couple of students snickered, which disconcerted me. I had not intended to be funny. "I'm so used to mixing dough to make two or three hundred Danishes, that generally I don't measure anything."

"See, Mrs. Jameson," the tall boy said, "she's a professional cook and she doesn't measure." The boy had long-lashed eyes stuck in a remarkably clear brown face.

Mrs. Jameson responded with a soft "Chendo," and a finger to her lips.

The beauty of Chendo's skin made him seem nerdy to me. Apparently stepping on a high school campus caused one to revert to stereotypes.

I hadn't looked forward to this presentation. Eldon, my boss, had pressured me to come, saying the demonstration would be good P.R. A reporter from the *Register Pajaronian* was supposed to be here. No such person was in evidence.

I yammered about "proofing the yeast," and smiled when some kid whispered about the muscles in my forearms, the result of years spent spiking volleyballs and stirring batches of dough.

I'd acquiesced to Eldon, the kitchen manager, for two reasons. First, it was useless to fight him on issues involving the image of Archibald's kitchen, where I was the main baker. I sighed. *Going on ten years. Most of my adult life.* Second, he'd hinted that there was a "mystery" for me to solve at the school, that Alvina Jameson wanted someone unofficial to "check into." I was flattered. I'd gained a reputation, at least among the kitchen staff, because I'd solved a murder case, but that had been over two years ago. I'd toyed with the idea of becoming a private investigator, but my husband Chad had been, and continued to be, dead set against it.

Eldon knew which buttons to push to get me to comply with his wishes. We had, though, compromised on my dress. I had agreed to wear the top half of our uniform, the white chef's jacket and chef's hat, if I could forgo the creepy hound's tooth pants for regular jeans.

"I don't think that's the right image," Eldon insisted. "It doesn't look professional."

"I'll believe I'm a professional," I replied, "when I get paid like one."

"That outfit would not accurately represent the way we dress at Archibald's."

"How am I going to check out this mystery for your *friend* if I stick out like a maraschino?"

His soft face twisted into a moue of disapproval. "Mrs. Jameson is not that kind of friend."

As I finished the Danish dough and hefted the bowl over to Alvina Jameson, I wondered how she and Eldon did know each other. I rolled the already cooled, manageable dough from the five-gallon bucket. The demonstration was going well. When I lapsed into silences, Alvina breezily filled them. "Look, class, at how she rolls the dough. A light touch."

"Do bakers make good money?" The boy who asked was as tall as Chendo, but filled out and beefy. He wore a red cap twisted backwards.

I felt like telling him that every twist of his cap shaved off I.Q. points, but instead I said, "No. I, fortunately, have a husband who works."

"Do you have any kids?" The girl was the one with the Godiva hair who'd set Chendo straight about my gender. She was so tiny only her chest and smooth, soft face showed above the table.

Alvina Jameson shot the girl a look to say the question was inappropriate, but the girl tipped her head of luxurious brown hair and gazed at me.

"I used to," I said dryly, "until I got this new recipe for pot pies." I enjoyed watching her figure it out. Her dark eyes popped. "I'll demonstrate that recipe next time Mrs. Jameson invites me to speak."

Eldon had supplied me with a generous two-quart container of expensive Danish filling, a mixture of marzipan, cream cheese, sugar, and slivered almonds. I brushed a thin layer onto the rolled dough, and sliced the dough into sixty strips.

"Do you always have to wear that dorky hat?" the beefy kid asked.

"Javier!" Mrs. Jameson scolded.

That was a hell of a question given his backward cap, but I kept my voice neutral. "It's either this *dorky hat* or a hair net." Thank God I'd won the argument with Eldon about the pants.

"I'd rather wear a hair net," he pushed.

"Not if you had all the hair I have." My braided mane hung down my back, any loose auburn wisps secured under the hat rim. I picked up one of the dough strips and twisted it like a locker room towel for snapping.

"Wow," Javier said sarcastically.

Mrs. Jameson edged close to his big shoulder. It didn't seem possible that she could intimidate him, but Javier wiggled, turned from her and wilted.

In about one second, I wrapped the dough around my forefinger into a Danish. I picked up another and another, fast as a machine, and I could see the kids grow suitably impressed. Chendo offered a genuine, "Wow." Showing off, I made Danishes with my eyes closed and then I shaped a few behind my back.

While my colleagues found such displays obnoxious, the kids liked it, and wanted to know what else I could do. After I'd dolloped each pastry with raspberry filling, the bell rang. I was tired, and nervous sweat bit my armpits, but I had to admit that I'd had enjoyed myself. Maybe I should become a cooking teacher.

CHAPTER 2

Alvina Jameson and I situated ourselves at a table of phony wood. A student had graffitied one corner. Alvina sighed, fetched a soapy paper towel, and scrubbed away the penciled XIV.

"I get so tired of this gang stuff." Although taller than my five-foot-eight, Alvina sat slightly lower in her seat. Her lined face suggested she was older than I was, so I assumed her hair had been dyed its even, dark brown.

We talked a little about how the presentation had gone as the aroma of baking Danishes filled the room. "I'm sorry about Javier's behavior." She picked a hair from her navy blue vest that matched her skirt and navy leather flats.

She served me a mug of fresh coffee and nodded at the pot. "There are advantages to being the cooking teacher." Her steaming white mug said: *Smile. There's a woman on the job.*

I shrugged. "I've met his type."

"It's not entirely his fault." She sighed. "I called home and had the displeasure of talking to Señor Garcia. Instead of listening to the problem, he wanted to know why the hell his boy was in a cooking class, as though I chose to have him here." She sighed again and ran a manicured fingernail below her eyes to wipe away any smudged mascara. While Alvina wore full foundation makeup and powder, her lipstick was a natural shade, her eyelids unadorned.

"The acorn never falls far from the tree." I groaned inwardly. One of my mom's platitudes had escaped my lips.

Alvina Jameson glanced away. "I shouldn't complain. I'm lucky this year to be able to stay in my room during my prep.

That's this period. Last year, a long-term sub taught in here during my prep. I can't imagine the class ever cooked. They literally festooned the tables with artwork."

When we returned to the topic of the demonstration, she felt that overall it had gone well. "I hope the personal questions didn't bother you?"

I reassured her that I didn't mind. "I hope the remark about baking my kids was okay."

Her smile was toothy and her brown eyes kind. I liked her and hoped that whatever she wanted was reasonable. "That's the nice thing about coming here as an outsider. You can say just about anything. As teachers, we have to be so careful. Especially now."

"What do you mean *especially now?*"

"I'm surprised that you haven't heard."

"I know nothing." I took off my chef's hat and unpinned my thick braid.

"Oh." She seemed at a loss how to begin. She glanced about the room as though to confirm we were alone, sidled closer in her chair, and whispered, "One of our most popular teachers, Richard Goicovich, has been charged with sexual harassment. He's on administrative leave until the end of the year."

"Who did he harass?" I heard my questioning and thought again what a good investigator I'd make. My husband Chad loathed the idea, but his worry was his problem.

"I'm not sure that he harassed anyone. That's the big controversy around campus. When I first heard the gossip about him and Jennifer Padilla, I kept waiting for the punch line."

"Who's Jennifer Padilla?"

"A student. A fabulous student, actually. Pretty. Smart. In the TAM program now." Her voice trailed off.

"Is this the matter that you wanted me to look into?"

"Oh no!" Her eyebrows shot up in alarm. "I mean, not really. Actually, it's important that no one know you're looking into anything. That's why I don't want a real investigator. Just someone, not myself, to poke into the situation."

"What situation?" The idea that Alvina did not regard me as a "real investigator" hurt my feelings, even though it was the simple truth.

The timer on the ovens buzzed, giving us a temporary diversion. We pulled the trays, put them on a rack, and left the Danishes to cool. Alvina snatched one, bobbling the hot pastry in her palm. Normally I didn't eat my product, but I figured that I'd better sample this time. She fetched pink paper napkins for each of us and refilled our coffee. The room was ringed with counters, sinks, stoves, ovens and cupboards, and a line of refrigerators. The tables in the center were battered, and the pattern was worn from the tile of the floor. The room had windows, but eggs, probably from Halloween vandals months ago, had spattered and dried on the exterior of the glass.

"Actually, I was hoping you could find out what happened with the cookies at the faculty meeting." She bit into her hot Danish with relish and munched, making appreciative "umms," and little nods.

"I'm lost," I said.

To test the sincerity of Alvina Jameson's approving sounds, I pinched a piece of warm pastry and nibbled it like a rat.

"Very good," she said, nodding.

Silently, I agreed.

"Last Wednesday, at the faculty meeting," she continued, "some of my kids sold cookies to raise money for our club. Peanut butter, oatmeal and chocolate chip. The class you just saw, third period, did the baking. Every teacher who ate a cookie got sick. Everyone thinks it was my class's fault, that we gave the staff salmonella poisoning or something."

"And you don't agree."

"Of course, I don't agree," she said hotly. "The idea of salmonella poisoning is ridiculous. The cookies were practically burnt because Javier had gone around turning up all the ovens."

"What do you think happened?"

"I don't know, but it crossed my mind that someone could have tampered with the dough."

"Poison?"

"Poison seems so cold-blooded. Maybe syrup of ipecac or another emetic."

"Well ipecac is poison. Of course, even baking soda is poisonous if you take enough, and it's hard to ingest enough ipecac to die because it causes vomiting." I was gibbering. Alvina Jameson's theory seemed farfetched and I didn't know what else to say. "Why would anyone sabotage the cookies?"

"Because of all the stuff that's been going on."

"The sexual harassment case?"

"That's one thing. This school has so many political undercurrents, the morale is so poor, and so many people are angry, that I hate to say it, but, yes, I think one of my colleagues could have . . . poisoned . . . the cookies."

This seemed paranoid to me. "Why a colleague?" I asked.

She sighed again. "I know, I know. Why not suspect a kid? They're so blamable. That would be easier. Someone like Javier. If he wanders around the room turning up the ovens, why not think that he's put something in the cookies? Because that's not his style. It's not immediate enough. Javier likes instant response. He's not into delayed gratification."

"What about another student?"

"You've seen the class," she said. "They're sweethearts. My best class. I hate to think it." She polished off her raspberry Danish and eyed mine.

"You'd rather believe a colleague did it?"

"I'd rather believe no one did it, but obviously something was wrong with the cookies. Everyone who ate one got sick—blurred vision, difficulty breathing, vomiting."

Alvina Jameson was right about one thing. The reaction was too sudden to be food poisoning. My demented personality included a fondness for reading about weapons and poisons. It stimulated me and kept my husband on edge.

"Ms. Salgado, that's our new principal, had to cancel the meeting. The library still stinks from the episode." With hardly a pause, she added enthusiastically, "The Danishes are delicious."

I pushed mine toward her.

"Are you sure?"

She barely waited for my nod. After chewing, she said, "I just don't believe the problem happened in my kitchen like everybody else believes."

"But it must have happened in this kitchen. The cookies were made and baked here."

"What I mean is that my class didn't cause the problem."

Of course not.

She sighed yet again. "I thought you were going to be on my side."

"How would another teacher get in here to doctor the dough?"

"That's not hard. We made the dough Monday morning and didn't bake the cookies until Wednesday, because the school had a special assembly Tuesday to give everyone an official non-explanation of Goicovich's leave to prevent a student uprising. Dick was Mr. Popularity."

Did I sense a trace of sarcasm?

"Watsonville High School had its centennial in 1992, and they say there's always been a Goicovich at WHS."

I suspected that I was getting into a situation stickier than biscotti dough. Chad would not be pleased. He'd hoped my first "case" would be my last. I'd been bopped on the head enough times he feared I'd wind up like Mohammed Ali.

Alvina listed ways other teachers could have entered the room. "The committee on school safety met here on Monday after school. If I go out for a while during my prep, I often leave the door open. Even if the door were locked, any teacher could get the custodian to let him in."

Now it was my turn to sigh. "So what you're suggesting is that nearly everyone had opportunity?"

"I'm also suggesting certain faculty members might have better motives than my students."

CHAPTER 3

When the bell rang, I jolted in my seat. "Aieee!" I cried in pain.

Alvina Jameson smiled. "The butt biter got you."

I scowled at the culprit, a crack in the bottom of the heavy blue plastic, and rubbed my cheek.

"That's what my kids call those cracks."

I was not amused. I wondered angrily if the California State Prison System had better chairs.

"Sorry. Around here we have to laugh or else we'll cry."

The other chairs had been stacked to make room for my demonstration, but I doubted they were any better. I sat down gingerly. "Do you have class now?"

"It's lunch time."

Buffalo stampeded the campus, the air thick with pounding hooves. A cacophony of slamming lockers and raucous voices halted our conversation.

When the door opened, the noise became a roar. "Mrs. Jameson," Chendo shouted, "could Belinda and me have a roll now?" Belinda was the tiny girl with Godiva hair, the crown at Chendo's sternum and the end of her hair down at her knees. The two wore matching black sweatshirts with gold tragedy and comedy faces on the front.

Alvina handed them the pastries on napkins. She didn't correct their English, but she did admonish them to wash their hands and reminded them that these were Danishes, not rolls. Again I wondered how she and Eldon were acquainted. If Eldon had a female friend, I'd imagine someone like Alvina with her small gold and pearl earrings and the high-collared white blouse sprigged with flowers beneath her vest.

Belinda turned from the sink, looking like a woman on one of those odious shampoo commercials who says, "Don't hate me because I'm beautiful." What she really said was, "Mrs. Jameson, this soap dispenser is empty." She and Chendo moved to the next sink and tried the dispenser there. "This one's almost out."

Alvina Jameson's lips pulled tight, and then she heaved her biggest sigh yet. Chendo said thanks, Belinda followed suit, and they hurried out the door, munching Danishes for lunch.

"How am I supposed to run a healthy kitchen with no soap?" Alvina asked. "Follow me."

We marched up the nearly vacant corridors and I marveled at how fast kids moved when inspired. All the buildings were painted various shades of dun and brown, with patches of not-quite-matched color where graffiti had been covered. We entered a dimly lit lounge, furnished with tables and couches that the Salvation Army would reject. Alvina and the brown baggers exchanged greetings. A bejeweled woman opened an avocado refrigerator, which emitted a stench of mold.

The teachers examined me as Alvina Jameson called the custodians' office. A guy who looked like a former football player stood near the phone, legs apart, hips aggressively forward. He flicked cold gray eyes down my body. I felt like I'd been unzipped. "So can this Rosendo wrestle?" he asked around a mouthful of tuna sandwich. He seemed to be addressing the bejeweled woman. "The other kids think he's a scrap."

"You're the coach, Ed," the woman replied, slapping her bag on the table. "You're supposed to help the kids become wrestlers."

In the slowed down, carefully enunciated voice one uses for answering machines, Alvina Jameson asked for a gallon of soap to be left in her room so that she could fill her own dispensers.

I could feel the eyes of the six teachers follow us as we departed. The door slammed behind us, the pneumatic hinge apparently long gone. "What's a scrap?"

"It's a derogatory term some Mexican kids call other Mexican kids," she said in a low voice. She stepped closer to me and whispered, "I've heard it refers to the scrap of skin from circumcision."

"Oh." It wasn't, I supposed, that different from calling someone an asshole.

"Leave it to Ed Smith to use a term like that." She sniffed as we reentered her domain.

I didn't know what to say to that, so I asked if Chendo and Belinda were a couple.

She shook her head. We sat and she finished her second Danish. "Only in the school play. Belinda is a cheerleader, very popular, from an old Watsonville family. White," she added. For the first time she eyed me skeptically, as though I might not be the person for the job, something I'd suspected an hour ago.

Her expression, however, made my intransigent perversity kick in. I was determined to solve the mystery even if it led right to one of Mrs. Jameson's darlings.

"They're both in *South Pacific*," Alvina continued. "Chendo is Joe Cable and Belinda is Bloody Mary's daughter."

"Chendo's good looking."

"Yes," she agreed. "But he's only a sophomore and Belinda's a junior. Cooking is an elective so the kids are all ages. Besides, Chendo's not cool."

At that moment I had one of those epiphanies that makes a person feel stupid. I realized what a literal word cool was. Chendo was not cool; he was warm and engaged. "You know that I'm not a private investigator."

"Yes, but I heard from Eldon how you solved that murder case at Archibald's and how you know a lot about poison. Actually, I don't want to hire anyone official. People already think I'm being ridiculous about this. They don't understand why I don't just accept responsibility for what happened. If they found out I brought in an investigator, they'd think I'd gone off the deep end."

Although Alvina Jameson was a likable person, and from what I'd seen, was a firm, competent, and kind teacher, the deep end idea had crossed my mind.

"Actually, hiring an investigator could probably jeopardize my job. On the other hand, if someone catches on to you, what are they going to say? There's nothing wrong with having a snoopy acquaintance."

I wondered if I were expected to volunteer my time and energy.

Reading my mind again, she said, "Eldon has graciously agreed to arrange three paid vacation days for you, if you'll look into this matter for me."

Boy, this woman did have some influence. She was dealing with an organization that didn't mind scheduling employees for six or seven days in a row, as long as they could slop the last days into a new pay period and thus avoid overtime.

I was more intrigued at the moment by her possible connection to Eldon, the big, asexual doughboy of a kitchen manager, than by her dilemma. If I found out anything at all, it seemed likely it would be that one of her students had played a prank, and that was not what she wanted to hear. Yet, I still hadn't relinquished the idea of surmounting my husband's objections and becoming a private investigator. Here was an opportunity not just gently knocking, but actually kicking down the door.

By the end of the lunch period, I left room 306 with a list of people Alvina thought I should talk to, where they were, their prep periods, a map of the school, a copy of Alvina's class roster, a huge doubt about her suspicions, and a growling stomach. I left by the street door, with all my accouterments loaded in the washed five-gallon pail. I tried to appear confident for anyone who might be peering out the grimy, egg-spattered windows and to the tardy students trickling back to the campus.

On a bright mural across the street, someone had spray painted huge penises on all the animals depicted in the scene.

The street sign told me this was Marchant. I'd been by here when working on the case Alvina had mentioned. I straightened my shoulders with a surge of completely illogical confidence, since I had no idea where my Karmann Ghia was in relationship to Marchant. I amused myself with the image of Tina Turner singing, "What's logic got to do with it?" On this side of the campus, scruffy grass had grown several inches onto the sidewalk, and an array of debris was caught in the indestructible juniper bushes, including what was either a jellyfish or a used condom.

As I neared the corner of the school, a tardy student stepped onto the sidewalk. Just the person I didn't want to see.

"Wadzup?" Javier said.

"You're heading the wrong way, aren't you?"

He shrugged, and pulled at the bill of the baseball cap at the nape of his neck. He wore a white tee shirt with three vertical creases ironed into the front that I was willing to bet he didn't make. The shirt billowed over his brown baggies, but his biceps filled the sleeves.

"Looking for your car?" he asked.

This time I shrugged. I didn't want this kid having any thoughts about my car. He probably would have considered anything less than a Camry with tinted windows a piece of crap, but to me, my rusted red '66 Ghia was a collector's item. "I'm starving. Do you know a good place to eat?"

He pointed up Beach Street. "Right across from the Plaza. Good burritos, carnitas, fajitas. You like Mexican food?"

"Love it."

He smiled, and I glimpsed the boy in him, just starting to get hair over his lip.

"Don't you have a class?" I asked as he fell into step beside me.

He shrugged again, his deltoids massive. Geez, Louise, I thought. What was this? I felt as if a pitbull had decided to follow me. So what if it were wagging its tail? He walked with me, but kept three body widths between us, as though to make clear he had no designs on my body, or so that no one would think that we were together. I managed to feel both relieved and insulted at the same time.

He waited at the newspaper dispenser as I went into El Charrito, a corner market with a Mexican food deli. I bought a chicken burrito. Javier trailed me across Beach Street to the Plaza, and when I sat on a park bench, he sat at the other end.

I tore open the bag and spread it over my lap. I lustily bit into the warm flour tortilla loaded with dripping, succulent chicken and immediately squirted a couple of beans and a drop of homemade salsa onto the waiting paper. I licked my fingers before the juice could drip down my arms.

At the end of the bench, Javier grinned as though he were personally responsible for the food. "Good?"

"Mmmm," I said, taking another unladylike bite.

"Mine are better."

I glanced at him to make sure I'd heard right, but he didn't meet my eyes. He gazed at his black boots. "My opinion, they don't use enough chilies." He took off his red cap. Leaning on his knees with his body angled away from me, he turned the cap over and over in his hands.

"I think I'd like to be a cook." His voice was barely audible.

CHAPTER 4

By the end of my burrito, I understood that Javier didn't have much idea what to do with his life. However, it had crossed his mind that he could cook, and he liked to cook, but the problem was his dad and his homies. They regarded this as totally uncool, women's work. "The only thing my dad thinks is okay is killing the goat. Maybe opening the beer." It also became apparent that Javier had no idea how to become a cook, and he thought I might be able to help him, either with advice, or better yet, a job.

I told him to stay in school and then to try to get into Cabrillo College's Culinary Arts and Hospitality Management program.

His forehead wrinkled as his brain chewed on the fancy words. He had the body of a senior, but the personality of a younger student. I guessed him to be fifteen.

"The majority of our cooks are men," I assured him.

I told him that I'd keep an eye out for an entry position at Archibald's. With the management's burn-and-turn philosophy of employment, jobs opened frequently. On the other hand, spots filled fast. "Nearly every employee has a cousin or brother who needs a job," I told him. I didn't want him to be too hopeful. Hope was a jester in a purple suit who juggled bright balls and occasionally tossed us one only to laugh if we dropped it.

I wanted to get back to the school to chat up some of the names Alvina had given me, but Javier seemed in no hurry to leave. It struck me that he had nowhere to go. He wasn't supposed to be at home, and the class he should have been attending was half over.

The plaza was certainly prettier than the high school. A walkway led from each corner of the block to a brick gazebo in the center. A couple of little kids played on its steps, and older people occupied most of the benches. Besides an orange-vested city worker tending to a display of primroses, everyone here appeared to be Mexican-American. To them, I was a gabacha. I looked white. I checked Caucasian on forms. My Spanish was learned in classes. If and when people thought about Sabala, my surname, they thought it must be my married name, or maybe Eastern European with an accent on the first syllable. They did not see my Mexican blood.

It was a mild March day. I would have liked to remove my chef's jacket, but knew I'd be too cold with only my dusty rose turtleneck. Javier must have been cold in his tee-shirt, but I held back comment, remembering myself in junior high, a shivering stick in mini-dresses that barely covered my buns, all just to have the right look. Well, hell, I thought, I'd ask Javier about some of the people Alvina had mentioned.

"So, Javier," I said with no pretense at smooth segue, "what do you think of Jennifer Padilla?"

He didn't look at me, but his whole body jerked up. "You know her?"

"I heard a little of the gossip."

"Yeah, well," he bent back over and resumed twiddling with his hat, "it's probably true what they say. That Mr. Goicovich harassed her. Got her pregnant, you know?"

"Jennifer Padilla's pregnant?" Why hadn't Alvina Jameson given me that bit of information? Then I realized that she probably had.

Javier made flicking eye contact. "I thought you knew her."

"Oh no," I back-pedaled. "I just heard the gossip." We were both being nicer to each other than we were naturally inclined to be. "Hey, Javier, what does TAM mean?"

"Teenage Mothers. That's the program Jennifer's in."

Ah so. That had been Alvina's delicate way of telling me that Jennifer was pregnant. Given the other information I'd received about the girl, I'd expected the acronym to stand for something like Terrific Academic Models. I needed to develop a more inquiring mind if I were to be an investigator. "Why do you think Mr. Goicovich was the one to get her pregnant?"

"Well, she says he harassed her."

"Harassment doesn't necessarily mean he had sex with her."

"Well, she's pregnant."

"Does Jennifer claim the father is Mr. Goicovich?"

"Well . . . no. She won't say nothing about who the dad is. Even her good friend Amy don't know."

"Do you know Jennifer pretty well?"

"Everybody knows Jennifer."

"What's your opinion of her?"

He twisted his head and his greenish brown eyes glittered with slyness. "*Firme*. She's fine."

I sighed in exasperation. "What about her personality?"

"She's fine," he repeated, as though I were dense as a burro. This seemed to mean fine as in fine wine.

If I questioned him hard enough, I might drive the kid back to school. Since his hostility had returned, I decided I might as well ask about the cookies.

"I didn't do nothing to the dough," he snapped. "Just like I told Mrs. Jameson, all I did was turn up the ovens."

"Why did you do that?"

"Bored."

"Is that what you'd do if you had a job in a real kitchen? What if you got bored up at Archibald's?"

His gaze fell down and away, but I could see his jaw muscles leap as he ground his teeth. I backed off. I'd had glimpses of the fifteen-year-old, but I still retained my initial impression of an explosive and powerful brute.

"Do you know anyone who might have put something in the dough?"

"No."

The answer seemed too fast and too unequivocal.

"Do you know what subject Jennifer has last period?"

"Why do you want to talk to Jennifer?" His eyes narrowed. "She don't take cooking."

I realized that not only had I put Javier on the defensive, but also I had no answer for his question. Although I'm a lousy liar by nature, experience had taught me that the best way to do it was to skim along the truth. "I'm a feminist," I said, "and I'm very interested in the sexual harassment case."

I might as well have said that I had a raging case of venereal warts and never washed my hands. He grimaced and scooted away another inch. "Don't you like guys?"

"I have a husband of whom I'm quite fond."

He pondered this imponderable. "I don't know Jennifer's last class, but her friend Amy has Goicovich, only now it's Mr. Reed."

"Amy?"

"Amy Hirahara."

I mentally practiced the name and then asked, "What do you think of Mr. Goicovich?"

He shrugged.

I wondered if the gesture were natural or adult-induced.

"Never had him. Some of my friends say he's cool. You can't blame a guy for hitting on Jennifer."

I not only could, I would, if the gossip were true. He was an adult. He was her teacher. I didn't care if Jennifer Padilla had stripped herself naked and hurled herself at him, he had a duty, a responsibility, a sacred trust to honor. Whew! I was glad I hadn't decided to spew this at Javier. It would have been like giving a teetotaler an intravenous fifth of vodka.

Maybe Javier sensed the inner furor. He jolted from the wooden bench, jammed his hat back on his head, and announced, "If I'm going to Cabrillo, I guess I better go back to school." He went down the sidewalk as fast as one could while maintaining a proper pimp stroll.

CHAPTER 5

It didn't take a Sherlock to figure out which student was Amy Hirahara. When the bell released the horde from room sixty-four, only three of them were Asian and only one of the three was female. She fortunately peeled from the crowd, jamming an arm through the strap of a blue backpack, so full that I could see the outline of two pens caught between the outermost book and the nylon.

"Looks heavy," I said.

She freed her long black hair from where it'd been pinned by the pack. "It is." Her eyes did a complete, unembarrassed inspection of me from thick braid down to my jeans and athletic shoes. "You must be the baker who did the demonstration for Mrs. Jameson."

That didn't take a Sherlock, either, as I was wearing my uniform top, but I was slightly surprised. This was a big school, as the hundreds of kids, walking in every direction across the concrete quad, testified. "Belinda gave me a bite of her Danish," Amy Hirahara explained. She was taller than Belinda, but probably didn't weigh an ounce more. She probably didn't weigh more than her backpack.

"Don't you have lockers for those books?"

She snorted. "If you want them rained on or stolen. Besides I have six egomaniacs who all think they're my only teacher. Besides, I'm Japanese. This is our image—four point o, and all that."

"Are you a four point o?" I asked.

"I have to be. Four point two, actually. If you're Asian, that's the only way you can get into a top university."

I followed her past a circular building that I knew from my map was the library, and toward the two-storied, gracious, brand new main building. It was painted a pale peach with forest green trim, vaguely Southwestern.

"I'm Yonsei," Amy griped. "Fourth-generation American, and I'll be lucky to attend a school for which I fully qualify."

We entered a courtyard. Above us large rubber snakes curled around the guardrails of the second floor's open air corridors. "Those are supposed to scare off the pigeons," Amy explained. "As you can see, they don't." Her ultra white tennis shoes tiptoed through bird droppings. These seemed less offensive to me than the gum droppings of students, big, dark, much less biodegradable splotches on the fresh concrete. I looked up again and shuddered at the snakes on the railings, not because I suffered from ophidiophobia, but because with the jostling crowds of kids, the design of the building looked like an accident waiting to happen.

Amy Hirahara opened a side door, and since I was still there, asked in a neither friendly nor unfriendly voice, "Are you lost?"

"No. If my deductions are correct, we are entering the Henry Mello Performing Arts Center."

Her delicate face wrinkled. "You're going to watch our rehearsal?" She took off her pack and plopped it into a cushioned, auditorium seat, the green upholstery plush and new. A cavernous stage loomed above us.

"Oh, you're in *South Pacific*, too?"

In way of answer, she puffed herself up and started to sing the betel nut song. The lyrics gave me an inexplicable, agitated feeling, like when I'm supposed to remember to do something, but I can't remember what.

"I'm Bloody Mary," she explained.

"Hiroshima!" a boy greeted Amy from the stage. He was tall and powerful for a high school kid. Buffed, was the teenage vernacular.

"That's Hirahara, asshole," Amy retorted.

"Hirahara Asshole," the boy said, "you're supposed to come in through the green room." He turned, and strode to the rear of the stage as though already gearing up for opening night.

Amy melodramatically swept hair over her shoulder.

"Who's that?"

"Arturo Arteaga." Her eyes sparked. "He's both smart and went to State in wrestling last year. Go figure. Not your stereotypical jock." Amy babbled, as though the very presence of the stage brought her to life. "He's our Emile, the only guy on campus who could sing *Some Enchanted Evening*, but if Coach Smith had his way, Arturo would only breathe wrestling."

As I followed Amy up the steps, she said in an enthusiastic stage whisper, "I wouldn't mind playing opposite him. 'Course me being Japanese, there wasn't any chance of that. It'd undermine the whole point of the play. Even Jennifer would have had to wear a wig." We crossed the wooden floor of the stage to the back.

"Jennifer was going to be the lead?"

Amy nodded. "That was before she got pregnant and Mr. Smith kicked her out of his P.E. class and she went into the TAM Program. She'd probably show by the time of the play, anyway, although I don't know how Smith knew she was pregnant, since she barely shows now."

We arrived at a large room behind the stage that buzzed with teenagers. "The green room," Amy said.

Green was an accent color throughout the building, but this room, ironically, was not green, but white.

"These rooms used to always be green," Amy said, "because green's a soothing color. It'd calm down the actors."

I recognized Chendo and Belinda from Mrs. Jameson's cooking class.

"Hiroshima!" Arturo commanded.

As much as Amy may have liked the hunk's attention,

she truly didn't like this nickname. "My name's Hirahara, butthead."

Arturo smiled, a dazzling sight. He seemed unaware how offensive the nickname might be. Was racism still racism when no malice lay behind it? I thought of my childhood when I called Brazil nuts "nigger toes." I cringed at the memory, but at the time I didn't even know the nuts had another name.

At that moment the teacher entered and snapped me from my reverie. She was as startled as I was to be staring at a familiar face.

CHAPTER 6

I knew Becky Rivas as a friend of my co-worker Patsy. Patsy was a body-building, Harley-riding, radical lesbian feminist. I quickly understood the flash of fear in Becky's green eyes. Watsonville was a conservative community, and she was not out of the closet. Not here. Not yet.

Becky plopped down an overstuffed woven bag. "Amy, what kind of language is that?"

"Is that the only thing you heard through the door?" Amy plucked up a grass skirt and shook it with a warning rattle. "Arturo was calling me Hiroshima, again."

"You know the new superintendent of schools might have walked in with me," Ms. Becky Rivas continued.

That, I thought, partly explained her prim attire--black silk blouse, denim skirt, nylons even, and black pumps. Or, maybe she always dressed this way in her role of teacher.

Amy's eyes narrowed to slits. She certainly lacked the girth to play Bloody Mary, but that could be faked with pillows. The girl tossed the skirt back onto a table. She possessed the right sense of power for the character. "Ms. Rivas, calling me Hiroshima is a racial slur."

"No, it's not," Arturo said in a deep, rich voice. "I don't call you Hiroshima because you're Japanese; I call you Hiroshima because you drop bombs." He didn't say, "So there," but the words hung in the air. This exchange may have been in high school vocabulary, but the dynamics hadn't changed from the sandbox.

The teacher's green eyes ping-ponged between the two. Other students drew near to witness the conflict. Becky Rivas had paled upon seeing me, and her color had not returned. Her freckles popped in high relief.

"Ms. Rivas," Amy appealed, "this is some kind of harassment, even if it's not sexual."

The allusion to sexual harassment threw the teacher's shoulders up to her ears. Arturo Arteaga took two menacing strides toward Amy. He was getting in Amy's face, although he had to bend over to do it. The other students ringed the scene, a captive audience.

Becky Rivas stepped boldly between the warring factions. "Baggage time!" she declared in a no-nonsense tone, and one by one the kids collapsed histrionically onto the floor in roughly a circle. Working on a drama production clearly created an intense and personal connection between the students and the teacher.

While the students were arranging themselves, Becky edged toward me until we were standing side by side. She wore Jean Nate and smelled nice. Sometimes I wished fragrances were allowed in the kitchen, and that I smelled like something besides vegetable oil and vanilla. "What in the world are you doing here, Carol?"

"Baking demo. Cooking class. But I need to talk to you about other stuff at the school. Can I call you?"

"Sure. But with rehearsals I'm hardly ever home."

"Can I listen in on this?"

She went through a mental debate. "It better be from the eaves."

I took her cue and acted as though I were leaving, even giving Amy a little wave, but stopping after I turned the corner to the stage. It wasn't hard to hear Arturo's big, booming voice. "Obviously, I have baggage," he said. "I really resent the way Amy and Jennifer got Mr. Goicovich fired."

"He didn't get fired!" Amy said viciously. "And I didn't have anything to do with what happened to him."

"Everybody knows how you cheated, Amy," the big voice sneered.

"I didn't cheat!"

The righteous indignation was so thick a person would need an industrial strength sponge to absorb it all. She either truly felt wrongfully accused, or she was one hell of an actress.

"See," the baritone said contemptuously. "That's just what I mean. You've never accepted that Goicovich caught you. You've been out to get him ever since it happened."

Tiny footfalls hurried my direction and I barely had time to conceal myself in the curtain as Amy Hirahara rushed by me, tears streaming down her face and her black hair flying. She pattered down the steps, retrieved her pack, and exited.

I'd followed Amy to rehearsal thinking that I might chat with her a bit about Jennifer and then to Chendo and Belinda about their cooking class, but everywhere I turned, I encountered the turbulence left in Goicovich's wake. Maybe there was something to Alvina Jameson's idea that the cookie poisoning was related to his dismissal.

I decided to call it a day. I knew one thing. Given a chance to turn back the clocks, I'd never return to being a teenager.

CHAPTER 7

On my way home, I dropped by Archibald's, my place of employment, a swanky conference center set on a eucalyptus-covered hill with a view over Santa Cruz to the Pacific. Eldon confirmed that I, indeed, had the next three days off if I agreed to help Alvina.

"Paid?"

The big, pudgy man nodded. As astounding as this was, as much as I wondered about Eldon's relationship to this cooking teacher, I nearly ran from the kitchen. This was as close as I'd come to being hired as an investigator. I pushed the Eurythmics' Greatest Hits into the tape player of my Karmann Ghia. Cranking up the volume, I sang off key at the top of my lungs.

In five minutes, I'd arrived at my tiny, two bedroom, one bath house located in the banana belt of Santa Cruz. March was not a great month for the perennials in the yard, although I did have white camellias and lilies blooming against the pale stucco. I stood in the street, peering into the regal palm, dramatic against the clouding sky, to see if I could spot our orioles. The fronds fanned my mind, trying to get me to remember something. I remained transfixed for so long that my cat Lola decided she'd better attack me. She pounced from one of the large rocks, did an uncharacteristic brush against my ankle, meowed in greeting, and followed me up the curved path of flat stones to the dark gray door.

I entered the house, debating whether to unplug the phone so that Eldon couldn't reach me if he changed his mind. Chad was smoking on the back landing. When he heard the front door open, he hastily ground the cigarette under his leather boot. As I slid open the glass door to the minuscule brick patio, he kept his boot planted on the butt. His action irritated me far more than the fact he'd been smoking. Did he think that I hadn't seen? And, even if I hadn't seen him, did he think that I couldn't smell the smoke?

"Hi, honey." He stood like a statue.

Did he plan to stay like that until I left, I wondered. I'd given up trying to reform Chad and had taken out a life insurance policy on him instead. He was an adult, and I wouldn't nag any of my friends the way I nagged him. On the other hand, I no longer had any friends who smoked.

Not moving his feet, Chad squatted and petted our super-intelligent, completely adorable, probably perfect, brindle cat. "How'd the demo go?"

In spite of the chilly weather, I settled myself in the glider. I feasted my eyes on Chad's James Dean looks as I gave him a synopsis of my day. His plaid flannel shirt worked loose from his jeans as he played with the cat. He scratched Lola's rump. Even though spayed, she arched her back and lifted her tail.

"She thinks that's foreplay," I said.

"Oh." He abruptly stopped petting Lola, retracting his hands as though they'd been slapped. He reminded me of the kids at the high school, the drama kids, with their exaggerated motions and emotions. Well, as a person who'd been abused as a child, Chad did have a lot of baggage. It was hard, though, when he took the simplest comment as criticism. I stood, stretched, and headed for the warmth of our tiny abode. Lola followed, and Chad made the caboose, kicking the cigarette butt into the flowers.

His subterfuge made me feel guilty; my harping had driven him to it. Communication certainly got convoluted fast in relationships. At least when Chad had smoked openly, he'd field stripped his cigarette butts, dropping the tobacco on the ground and pinching the paper into a wad to dispose of in a garbage can. Chad settled glumly on one of the caned chairs at our drop-leaf maple table.

"What's the matter?" I asked, moving to the kitchen area, which was just the other side of the room in our small house.

"Nothing." He turned his doleful blue-green eyes toward me. Chad possessed the hard, tanned body one might expect of a roofer, but today the hardness extended up his face—square jaw, tight eyes, strained forehead.

"Did Mary have to go back in the hospital?" As soon as I said it, I chastised myself with my mother's proverb, "A fool's mouth is his destruction." There was a force in me that wouldn't accept "nothing" for an answer, that always had to get to the bottom of things. I couldn't, as my mom would say, "let well enough alone."

"What do you care?" Chad said testily.

That was a deserved and provoked response. I cared about Mary only in as much as she affected Chad. In truth, I considered her an ogre. I refused to think of her as Chad's mother, since she'd literally abandoned him to her parents. Chad called her Mary because he'd grown up calling his grandmother Mama. I picked up Lola for some comfort, but she meowed in protest, twisted, and leaped from my arms. Independent. A Norman Rockwell print at my vet's office depicted people with pets resembling themselves. Did Lola mirror me?

"Mary fell again," Chad explained.

The best thing was to let him talk and not to offer sympathy, which he'd think was false. I poked in the refrigerator for something that might be magically transformed into dinner.

"Yeah, what is for dinner, Carol?"

What is going on?

"I didn't have any time to go shopping," he continued in his aggrieved voice.

My blood pressure rose. I could feel my heartbeat in the bridge of my nose. Chad was taking Mary's indirect, martyred tone. I told myself not to say that. Practicing great restraint, I said, "No one asked you to go shopping, Chad." It came out sounding as pissed off as I felt.

"Oh. Well. What's for dinner then?" He tried to keep his voice neutral, but it had a decidedly nasty edge to it. I moved things around in the refrigerator. "Let's see. How about . . . pickle relish, and . . . moldy cheese, on . . . " I scooted aside a heel of bread. " . . . on tortillas," I finished brightly. I whirled with a grin. He was not smiling.

"If you want me to cook, at least you could shop, instead of running around pretending to be a private investigator."

I froze, and imagined what a weird blunt instrument a cutting board would make. I sorted through the layers.

"We can order a pizza or get Thai take out," I offered.

But Chad knew that. This was not about what we'd eat for dinner. It was about time, and how he didn't have any because after roofing for ten hours, he ran and jumped to his mother's real and imagined problems. She'd been in and out of the hospital at least five times in the last month. But, since he had a major blind spot in this area, he was taking out his frustration on me, implying that I should have been home taking care of my share of the household responsibilities instead of going off on another wild goose chase.

And underneath all of this was worry. Mary's possible mortality made Chad frantic, aggravating his possessive nature, so that he wanted to grab on to me and cling. The last thing he wanted was for me to risk my life.

I decided to cut to the chase. "Look, this case isn't even dangerous, just kids pulling a prank with cookies. No one has even been killed."

"Not yet," he grumbled.

In the next three days, I'd wonder at least a dozen times what made him say that.

CHAPTER 8

I appeased Chad with dinner at the Real Thai Kitchen on Seabright Avenue, a few blocks from our house. We walked, in spite of the weather. After what had shaped up to be another winter of drought, March had arrived with rain. And more rain. The restaurant was a hole-in-the-wall, one unit of a strip mall. It had a few tables in the front smoking section, and about a dozen tables in the back non-smoking section.

A tiny Thai woman, wrapped in a peachy silk sarong, greeted us, menus in hand.

"Nonsmoking, please," Chad said.

I felt myself relenting, my heart opening again. Sitting in non-smoking was one of many concessions he made for me.

On this dreary weekday, we shared the place with only two other couples. We ordered jasmine tea, Gaeng Kour with chicken, Pad Tao Hou San Rod, and steamed white rice to cool our mouths after eating the curry and tofu with jalapeños. On his second plateful of the sinus-clearing food, Chad begrudgingly volunteered, "Mary cracked her hip."

Even though the Thai didn't use chopsticks, I'd requested them. I lowered a succulent piece of curried eggplant into my mouth. Partly to keep it closed. A cracked hip was serious. Big-boned and rotund, Mary was an unlikely candidate for osteoporosis, but in an article on that subject, I'd read that a cracked hip often began a woman's demise. On average, the article said, women lived only six months after cracking a hip. I didn't tell Chad this, but I wondered what our lives would be like without Mary. I shoved rice in my mouth.

On television I'd seen a program featuring an authority on family dysfunction. He'd had a large mobile on stage to illustrate how members of a family assumed roles to keep the whole in balance. The roles weren't healthy, so the family was termed dysfunctional, but given their remarkable adaptations in order to function, the term seemed a misnomer. Remove a piece, and whoa.

As soon as we were home, Chad called Dominican Hospital, so it was eight o'clock by the time I got to make the call I wanted.

"You've reached the home of Becky Rivas and Shayla Ivankovich."

"Hello," a real person said, out of breath.

"Becky?"

She shut off the recording. "Who's this?"

"Carol. Carol Sabala. Did you just get home?"

"Yup." I heard noises that suggested she'd sat down and kicked off her shoes on to a hard floor. "And I have papers to correct."

I'd thought that teachers had it good with summers off, but one demo for thirty-five kids had exhausted me, and that was with Alvina doing the managing. I remembered the scene Becky Rivas had stepped into after school, and the woman still had papers. I scratched teacher off my list of alternative careers.

"Do you have a minute to talk?" I asked.

"Actually, no."

I was so used to Chad's indirection that such bluntness caught me off guard.

"Could I talk to you tomorrow?"

"When?"

"Do you have a prep period?"

"Sure. But I'll be in and out of the office."

"I'll find you."

"You'll be at the school?" she asked. "Why are you going to be at Watsonville High? What's going on, Carol?"

I could have asked Becky Rivas the same question. She sounded too defensive. "I have another cooking demo." This was a lie and was met with a stiff silence. If I were going to snoop around for Alvina Jameson, I would need a cover. I'd better talk to Alvina about blending me into her curriculum for the next few days, and to Eldon about supplying the necessary materials. "So, could I talk to you tomorrow?"

"What about?"

"Some of the stuff going on at the high school."

"Like what?"

"Well, like the cookies that made everybody sick."

Becky guffawed. "What a mess!" Her voice relaxed. "I, fortunately, didn't eat any. What's Alvina been telling you about that?"

I avoided the topic. "I'd like to find out the scuttlebutt about the sexual harassment charge, too."

"Why do you want to know about that?"

It was time to take the offensive. "Why don't you want to talk about it, Becky?"

Becky let the silence stretch. Then she said tiredly, "I have fourth period prep. I'll be on the stage."

CHAPTER 9

I arrived at Watsonville High School at 7:30 a.m., a leisurely start to the day compared to baking by 4 a.m. I'd planned to talk strategy with Alvina before school, but I drove around the school two times looking for a parking place, and finally, unhappily, parked my Ghia, my poor woman's Porsche, three blocks away in the surrounding neighborhood. After I met Alvina at her room, I had to run to keep up with her, first to the main building to pick up her bulletin, attendance sheets, and other mail. She popped up a big black umbrella to protect us both from the morning drizzle. She'd be delighted to have me take over her cooking classes.

"Classes?"

"First and third."

I trotted behind her through a side door of the library into a tiny room occupied by a hulking copying machine that stapled, collated, and from the line and air of urgency, determined teachers' days.

"I have to run off a quiz," she explained. "Actually, the quiz is about your presentation. Name of the pastry, how to proof the yeast, that kind of thing. Less pedagogical than classroom management."

My expression must have said *huh*, because she closed the umbrella and continued. "I give lots of simple quizzes so kids get the message that they have to be in class and pay attention to pass."

She introduced me to the three teachers in line as "Carol

Sabala, a baker from Archibald's, who'll be working with me the next few days."

I recognized the woman named Hortencia Gonzalez from yesterday's trip to the teachers' lounge. She was short and dark, wore lots of jewelry and tapped her red nails on the plastic of the machine as she waited for it to finish spewing her copies. The tall, blonde second woman made the two together a study in contrasts. The third person was Ed Smith, the wrestling coach Amy Hirahara had mentioned, also familiar to me from the teachers' lounge. He stood apart from the two women with his arms crossed over his chest, and made an almost imperceptible nod to acknowledge the introduction.

Hortencia asked Alvina if she'd figured out what went wrong with the cookies.

"No."

"I still don't feel good," Hortencia said.

"I can still smell it," the other woman griped.

I caught the scent drifting in from the reading room of the library, the residual, bitter smell of vomit, and the cloyingly sweet smell of the stuff used to clean it up.

"Do you think we'll have to make up the faculty meeting?" Hortencia Gonzalez asked. This apparently was a fate worse than food poisoning, and angry speculation distracted the two women from the topic of the cookies.

Hortencia glanced at her watch and rushed away with her papers. The blonde woman stepped up to bat. The room had the atmosphere of the NASA control center during countdown.

Alvina had written Ed Smith's name on the list of people that I should interview. He was Richard Goicovich's buddy on campus, and her theory was that someone had tampered with the cookies because of Goicovich's dismissal. Ed Smith taught P.E. and looked the part. I estimated him at six-foot-two, tall for someone who, according to Alvina, had been a wrestler in his glory days. He wore black sweats with a hooded top and a gold Wildcatz emblazoned on the front. His rugged face, slightly scarred, was made handsome by a strong chin and chiseled lips. He exuded pheromones.

No time like the present, I thought, and hated myself for thinking in adages like my mom, although my mom was much more of the haste-makes-waste school.

"So, Ed. . . ."

The man whirled toward me. Gray eyes flicked me up and down. He smiled faintly as though the inspection had proven satisfactory.

"As a man," I made the word as salacious as I could without sounding false, "how do you feel about this sexual harassment scandal?"

I felt, rather than saw, Alvina cringe while the other woman's ears perked so high they pulled her body upright.

Ed Smith drew himself up. He could have had a thought bubble over his head full of exclamations and stars and pound signs. He was a man's man, the type of guy who'd have a five o'clock shadow at four o'clock.

"Where have you been hearing about that crap?" His granite eyes glared at Alvina.

"Not from Alvina," I said. "I'm a regular citizen who reads the paper."

"And I'm the tooth fairy."

After checking the clock three times to make sure she really had to miss this unfolding drama, the blonde teacher gathered her papers and left the room.

Ed Smith punched his code number into the copying machine and turned his back to me.

"So you don't believe the charges?"

"Pure, unadulterated bullshit," he said, turning to face us. Alvina Jameson shrank to my height, and moved behind my back.

"So, you think Jennifer Padilla is some sort of pathological liar out to ruin Richard Goicovich's career?"

For all his big, intimidating maleness, our Mr. Ed Smith looked a tad-bit pale. He jabbed at a button to clear his code from the copying machine. As Alvina scurried up to run her quizzes, Mr. Ed stepped over to me. A little too close. His eyes were flinty. "Let me tell you something." His neck muscles bulged.

"I'm listening." He didn't like this response. I guess he expected complete, submissive silence.

"Since you feel determined to get in my face . . . "

If he hadn't been so big and angry and close, I would have laughed at the irony.

". . . let me tell you that I don't have a clue what goes on in that girl's head, but I've known Dick for twenty-eight years, and yes, it is easier for me to believe that she's a pathological liar than it is to believe Dick Goicovich is guilty of sexual harassment. I don't know what you women are trying to accomplish, but pretty soon guys are going to be afraid to talk to you."

"What a relief." If this was Ed's idea of conversation, I could live without it.

He turned brusquely and strode out the door.

CHAPTER 10

"Eldon said you had balls," Alvina told me, as I galloped behind her across a dirt area by the English wing. I moved like a cobra to stay in the protection of her swaying umbrella. A deafening bell rang, and we dodged around kids. They coalesced out of nowhere into mobs on the walkway. The students dawdled compared to Alvina Jameson.

"Eldon said that?" I was pleased, but Eldon saying "balls" was more surprising than Alvina repeating it.

I don't think she heard me over the noise. The crowd smelled like wet wool. She slowed and lowered her voice. "It's no wonder Ed reacted that way. Ever since Anita Hill, he's been afraid some girl will come out of his past."

"A student?"

"When I first started here, there were rumors about him. But he cleaned up his act after his second wife left him." A couple of kids waited at Mrs. Jameson's door.

"How do you and Eldon know each other?" I asked.

Alvina's brown eyes twinkled. "That's our little secret." She propped her umbrella in the metal garbage can inside the door and removed her tan raincoat. Underneath she wore a lavender blouse and floral-print skirt.

She greeted students as they trickled into the Home Ec room.

The final bell rang and they continued to arrive. "Isn't there a consequence for being tardy?"

She sighed. "I can assign detention, but if a kid doesn't report, it'll be weeks before the office tracks him down.

They'll then give the kid Saturday School, and if he doesn't show for that, it'll take them another three weeks to track that down. The kids know this, so few of them serve detentions, which means that assigning detention only starts a useless paper trail."

"Why don't you assign them detention with you?"

Alvina scowled. "You mean punish myself because the students are late?"

I hadn't thought of it that way. "You need a detention center."

She smiled wanly. "Yes, we do. We also need counselors, a librarian, and more custodians."

A person didn't have to push hard to strike a nerve with these teachers. I'd keep my ideas about running the school to myself.

In theory this class was the same as third period, but the students yawned at Alvina as she read the bulletin. Some seemed unable to lift their heads from the tables. As a person who's at work by four, I couldn't bear this.

Kids continued to arrive for the next fifteen minutes. "Don't they have bed times? Curfews?" I whispered as the students took their quizzes on whatever they'd studied yesterday.

Mrs. Jameson shrugged. "I doubt it."

After the quiz, Mrs. Jameson introduced me and told the students that I'd be giving baking demonstrations for the next two days.

"What are you going to show?" a girl asked shyly. She had a dark braid down her back and a thick accent.

Without thinking, I picked what was easiest and would most likely be available from Archibald's. "Cookies."

"Coo-kies?" The girl's dark eyes widened, and she looked to Mrs. Jameson for confirmation. "Are we really going to make cookies?"

Mrs. Jameson nodded. "In spite of what happened at the faculty meeting, I am completely confident in your ability to make cookies."

"I wish my other teachers felt that way," the girl said sadly.

"Have they been giving you a hard time, Josephina?" Mrs. Jameson asked.

Josephina nodded.

"I can't believe this," Mrs. Jameson said. "Your class didn't even bake the cookies!"

The interchange reminded me of my purpose. The vomit-inducing cookies were easy to forget in the tumult of the sexual harassment charge. Only Alvina Jameson's hunch, probably a serious case of denial, linked the two. Any of her students, not just from third period, but from this class, or any of her classes, might have poured an emetic into the dough. I felt a moment of despair. A high school, especially one with over two thousand students, was an extremely complex society, partly a microcosm of the community, and partly as secret and exclusive as the Masons. I didn't feel I could understand it in three days. I wasn't sure an outsider could understand it at all, much less unravel a mystery contained within it.

I inspected the sleepy group. They seemed incapable of tampering with cookie dough except in their lingering dreams.

Second period, Alvina Jameson taught sewing. She assured me that none of her other classes had any business near the refrigerators, and that she would have noticed if any student had even opened a door. I left to interview Jennifer Padilla in the TAM Program, which Alvina this time mentioned stood for Teenage Mothers.

"Be careful," Alvina cautioned as though I were setting off into land-mined territory.

I raised one eyebrow. My ability to do that and to outstare just about anyone were two of my detective skills.

"Mrs. Goicovich, that's Viola Goicovich, runs that program."

I paused to digest this. "Jennifer Padilla, who's accused Richard Goicovich of sexual harassment, and who's currently pregnant, is in a program run by the man's wife?"

She nodded solemnly. "And Jennifer doesn't have to be in that program. It's not mandatory that pregnant girls take TAM."

"Why is she there? That's insane."

"It's tense," Alvina agreed.

The worn steps of the portable gave the place a look of permanence. Inside, the tension was so palpable it vibrated the walls. However, the appalling number of girls diffused the strain.

"There's no stigma anymore," Viola Goicovich explained. She was a woman beyond Rubenesque who wore a sleeveless, purple silk blouse on a day when the girls were bundled in sweatshirts and jackets. Purple barrettes above each ear held back full, curly-as-only-natural-can-be, blonde hair. Chunky, colorful earrings and necklace popped her chocolate eyes into high relief. A multi-colored skirt swayed like a hula girl's as she handed back homework to the girls in various stages of pregnancy. Fat Viola was; dowdy she wasn't. "Most of Santa Cruz County is below the state average in pregnancy rate, but when they figure in South County, we shoot up above the state average." She said this in a normal voice, for all the girls to hear.

She needed to get on with her teaching. "Jennifer," she snapped, without looking at the girl. "Jennifer Padilla." She waved a paper into the air.

When Javier had called Jennifer Padilla "fine," I hadn't expected to have the same opinion. I don't know what I'd expected, someone more fashionable and made up, I guess. The girl walking toward us wore no make up. She didn't need it. She had flawless, pale skin and was exotically, and unpretentiously, beautiful.

"This lady would like to speak to you," Viola Goicovich informed her. She didn't even glance at the girl, and her voice was cold.

"Can we go outside?" I asked.

Viola Goicovich nodded curtly, as though glad to be rid of Jennifer Padilla, and the girl followed me without protest, as though glad to escape. The rain had stopped for the moment, but the plum-colored clouds promised more.

Next door was another portable building that appeared equally permanent. Beside it a small, deserted playground held plastic structures and tiny slides for toddlers. Jennifer popped into the building and returned with paper towels. We wiped off opposite sides of a picnic table and perched atop fresh squares of paper towel.

The girl didn't look pregnant. She wore baggy jeans and a Yale sweatshirt.

"Yale?" I inquired.

"I hope so."

"What about the baby?"

"I'm due in August, and I'm giving up the baby for adoption."

Her calmness and sureness took my breath away.

"Aren't you afraid that you might change your mind?"

"No." Dark, thick hair, cut into a classical page, fell forward, and she swiped one side behind an ear. Her voice was pleasant and her poise remarkable. She added nothing to her simple answer.

How did such an assured girl get pregnant in the first place? I asked.

"Birth control isn't infallible." The cat-like shape of her eyes suggested a possible Asian ancestor. The eyes snapped with intelligence. "And who are you to be asking all these questions?"

"Carol Sabala." It didn't seem to me like Alvina and I were fooling people, so I told Jennifer the truth. "I'm snooping around for Mrs. Jameson to find out what happened to the cookies at the last faculty meeting."

The girl smiled. "She's a nice woman."

"I hear a 'but' on the end of that."

"But why doesn't she accept that one of her precious angels did the deed?"

"Like who? Do you have an idea about who might have done it?"

"Not really."

"But maybe?"

She shook her head. I had a feeling, though, that she did know something. 'Not really' was an equivocal response.

"How do you know Mrs. Jameson?" I asked.

"She and her sewing classes are helping to make the costumes for the play."

"*South Pacific*. You must be disappointed not to be a part of that."

She sang in a sweet, clear voice that she couldn't work herself up to feeling low. I'd seen the movie *South Pacific* years ago, and her tune jumpstarted my memory of the story.

I was spellbound. The response had been quick and apt. I definitely was not sitting with any ordinary high school senior. "Encore."

She smiled, stood, tweaked out her baggy jeans as though they were a skirt, and danced in the confines of the playground as she sang another song from the play.

Her voice was not big or full like Arturo Arteaga's, but it was true as spring water. When she sat down, flushed and smiling, I asked, "So who's the wonderful guy you're in love with?"

"Oh no," she demurred. "That's just from the play. I was going to be Nellie. You know, Mitzi Gaynor's part. Nellie's in love with Emil." The incredible, poised Jennifer Padilla was flustered. "But a person can't have everything."

Have everything? What an odd thing to say. What had she gained in place of the play except a baby that she planned to give up? "What about the father of the baby?"

She rose abruptly, and her Cleopatra eyes skewered me. "The father of this baby is absolutely nobody's business."

The topic was so repellent it drove Jennifer Padilla right back to that room containing her nemesis, Viola Goicovich.

CHAPTER 11

I loathed cloudy weather that refused to break into rain. It left a person feeling frustrated—promised and denied.

If I were a skilled investigator, I berated myself, I wouldn't have popped that question about the father of the baby. People had warned me that Jennifer wouldn't reveal his identity. I must have a monumental ego if I thought she'd tell me, a stranger.

I crossed a street, which segregated the fields, the Ag and Industrial Arts Buildings, Teenaged Mothers, and the program for the "challenged" students from the rest of the campus.

I hadn't even touched on Jennifer's sexual harassment charge. And I had no lead on who had messed with the cookies.

The concrete quad, an extension of the new building, had square openings in it, which I hoped meant trees were on the way. Right now the area looked stark as a parking lot. Students started to spill from the classrooms though the bell hadn't rung. Then it did ring and hordes flooded the concrete plain.

I reached the safety of Alvina Jameson's room.

"How's it going?" she asked.

"Crummy. So to speak." I inspected one of the blue plastic chairs for cracks and plopped into it.

"I don't expect anyone to 'fess up. I just feel like I owe it to my students, and to myself, to do this." Alvina galloped to the sink and filled her mug with tap water, hurried back to erase the board, and began a frenzied search of her desk. "Did you see where I set period three's quizzes?" She found them too quickly for the question to be anything but rhetorical. She looked at the papers instead of at me. "Maybe I should stop this investigation. Everybody thinks I'm being ridiculous."

I sweated like a junkie denied a fix. "Do people know that you've hired me?"

"No. It's not that, they just think. . . ." She twirled her hands inarticulately.

Since I hadn't been obligated to wear my chef's uniform today, I wore a black jacket, which kept me toasty. I unsnapped it, but felt no relief from the flush of my body. I was addicted to the hunt. I did not want Alvina Jameson to change her mind about this investigation even though I thought she'd receive bad news at the end.

Students entered, including Chendo, who was singing in the unselfconscious way most people reserved for the shower. His song was the one about being taught to be afraid of people who are different. Chendo stopped abruptly as though he'd forgotten the next line.

I'd thought *South Pacific* a goofy, schmaltzy choice, especially for someone like Becky Rivas. If I remembered right, the musical had given us *Nothing Like a Dame*. Now I remembered the musical's other, more serious, theme, the one of racial prejudice.

The lanky boy stopped walking when he spotted me. "What are you doing back?"

Alvina explained to the students in general that I'd be giving another demonstration tomorrow and Thursday.

"Since I won't be demonstrating today," I whispered when she was done, "I guess I'll get on with the investigation."

She didn't scream *no*. She'd apparently been expressing doubts rather than a change of heart. The bell rang. If I had a gun, I would have shot the damn thing. Here people moved, sat, talked, ate, and probably went to the bathroom according to a bell schedule. It would, I thought, drive me crazy, and the students, like Javier, who sauntered in at his own pace, might have the right idea.

"Javier, what are you chewing?" Alvina asked.

The boy didn't answer, but rather walked to the garbage can by the door, opened his mouth, and released a huge blob of gum.

I had a niggle at my brain stem. The scene had hatched an idea, and its delicate wings fluttered against the inside of my cranium. From experience I knew that grabbing at this elusive idea would crush it. I had to allow it to arrive at its own time.

"Is there any way that I could talk to Goicovich?"

"Given the nature of his leave," Alvina whispered, "he's not allowed on campus during the school day, but the administration has made provisions so that he can come after school and clean out his room."

"That sounds drastic. Like he won't be back."

Alvina shrugged her lavender shoulders. "It does give a person that impression."

"Guilty until proven innocent?"

She shrugged again and addressed the class. "Take out a sheet of paper. We're having a quiz on Ms. Sabala's presentation." A couple of kids chirped that they hadn't been there yesterday. "That's too bad," she said with genuine regret. "There's no way to redo the demo, so I suggest that you take the quiz, making your most intelligent guesses."

She was a tough cookie. I left the room and found a bathroom. It was dark, partly from the density of the graffiti. The first stall had no toilet paper. The second stall had a bloody pad on the floor, and the third stall had something nasty on the seat. There were no toilet seat covers, so I opted for the second stall.

The water in the sink was cold only and there was no soap. I reached for a paper towel. The dispenser was empty. This could be the reason the faculty had gotten sick from the cookies. I shook water from my hands, my brain full of unprintables, and dried my hands on my jeans.

I sat at one of the picnic benches in the dirt area by the English wing, positioning my butt on the tail of my coat to protect it from dampness. A huge pine had cushioned this area with dried needles and probably accounted for why the area was left bare.

I studied the names and places Alvina had given me the day before. I could see why Alvina Jameson had not taken a definite stance on the charge against Richard Goicovich. Having met Jennifer Padilla, it was difficult to imagine the remarkable, pretty, Yale-bound girl had made up stories to ruin the career of a respectable, middle-aged man. Why would she do that? Yet, people from student Arturo Arteaga to Goicovich's buddy Ed Smith reacted hotly to the charges. Arturo had even suggested the charges were some sort of plot dreamed up by Amy and Jennifer. Jennifer motivated by the harassment and Amy by some sort of cheating accusation.

Sides seemed to have been drawn along gender lines. I wondered what Viola Goicovich thought. I needed to talk to her. "Use some finesse this time, Sabala," I admonished myself as I rested for a moment longer at the picnic table.

In the past two years, after solving the murder at Archibald's, I'd dabbled in a lot of things to test my interest in becoming a private investigator. I'd had a friend of Chad's teach me to fire a gun which had confirmed that I didn't like guns, although I wasn't that bad at using one. I'd taken a class in Criminal Justice at Cabrillo, the local junior college. I'd learned about street drugs and pedophiles and organized vs. disorganized killers. All of that had been interesting, but I'd deduced that my real attraction to this sort of situation was the human puzzle.

"Hello, Ms. Sabala."

I jumped about a foot. "Chendo! What are you doing out of class?"

He waved a green pass at me. "Bathroom."

"Whew," I said. "You're brave." I gestured toward the girls' room. "I was just in that one."

"Why didn't you use a teacher bathroom?"

Because I hadn't thought of it, which verified what my mother said about me, that I'd get so caught up in my thoughts that I'd forget to tie my shoes.

Chendo sat backward on the picnic bench, elbows on the table. One Nike jiggled up and down on the ground so violently that the whole picnic table vibrated.

I had the distinct impression that a revelation quivered on the horizon. The boy drummed both thighs. "Coming to our rehearsal tonight?"

I hadn't thought about it, but that depended on what I found out today. "Maybe."

"There's trouble right here in River City," Chendo said, looking straight ahead at the dun-colored buildings. He sat with me the way Javier had. Anyone passing would doubt we were together. It imbued the ordinary picnic bench and minimalist landscape with cloak and dagger tension, especially given Chendo's jumpy state.

"You mean the poisoned cookies?"

One long calf bopped as though it'd received a reflex test. The boy blanched. "I meant the stuff about Goicovich and Jenn. How could they get rid of Goicovich? Is that legal?"

Why is this boy asking me about legality? Who or what did he think I was? Obviously not just a baker.

"He's the best teacher I ever had." Chendo's voice caught. "When I was a freshman, he prevented me from committing suicide."

Chendo seemed to believe that I had some power to affect Goicovich's fate. I hated to dissuade a young person who'd once been suicidal, especially one whose nervousness was making the picnic bench feel like a low-budget ride at the Boardwalk.

"See, my brother's a gangster."

I didn't see at all, but since Chendo was actively not looking at me, he wasn't picking up non-verbal clues.

"Red 'til he's dead."

"A Northsider?" I knew something about the Watsonville

gang scene from the employees in Archibald's kitchen and from my last bit of sleuthing.

"The way I am," Chendo said mournfully, "I may as well be a faggot as far as my homies are concerned. To them a play is as bad as ice-dancing."

Slowly, I realized that Chendo was explaining why he'd been suicidal. If being thought homosexual were that bad, what was it like at this school for those who actually were gay? The memory of my brother Donald ambushed me. It had a way of leaping from behind stop signs, jumping from Ben and Jerry's Cherry Garcia ice cream, or fluttering on notes of Doo-wop. Donald had died from AIDS, but even after four years, I was never prepared for the attacks, and they pierced my heart. They turned me inside out like an emptied pocket.

Chendo continued morosely, "Everybody blames Jenn for Goicovich's dismissal."

Chendo's conversation was bouncing as nervously as his leg. He may not have been currently suicidal, but he was fragile. In my softest, calmest voice, I ventured, "But Jennifer *is* responsible for the sexual harassment charge, isn't she?"

"Not the way people think. They go around spreading rumors that Mr. Goicovich got her pregnant. That's not true!" He twisted around. The long-lashed eyes gazed at me. "I know it's not." He bit his lip.

Did that mean that he knew who the father was? Was he trying to defend Goicovich or Jennifer? Or both? For someone who cared about both people, this had to be a harrowing situation. He turned around as though he found the scarred, dark brown door into room sixty endlessly fascinating. I could not converse this way. Maybe that was the whole idea. For the second time in one day, I felt as though a male wanted me to be a receptacle, a passive vessel into which to pour his woes, or, in Ed Smith's case, his wrath.

"I know Mrs. Jameson doesn't think any of us messed up

the cookies, but what do you think?" Chendo asked.

What I thought was that Alvina and I had not been subtle enough. This boy seemed perfectly aware of my real purpose. "I haven't reached any conclusions. Do you know something that might help us?"

His bounce from the seat was an extension of all the little bouncing he'd been doing. "I better get back to class."

I watched him retreat down the covered corridor. He walked with the stiffness of someone who knows he's being watched. He wore baggy jeans and a No Fear sweatshirt, but Chendo was afraid. Since he hadn't used the bathroom, I gathered he'd come out here to find me. He'd meant to tell me something. I didn't have to dig deep to know what had prevented him. Teenagers didn't squeal. You didn't betray your peers to adults. Nothing was more uncool. And Chendo yearned to be cool, since he simply was not.

Chendo, Javier, and Jennifer all knew more than they would tell, and unfortunately for Alvina, that made me think that one of the kids had laced the cookie dough.

I examined the schedule again. There was no one with third period free that I wanted to interview. I walked around the English wing to room sixty-four, Mr. Goicovich's room, on the Beach Street side of the campus. All the English classrooms had a string of windows, high in the walls where no one could see in or out of them. I peered through the glass slit in the door. In front of me a group of boys played hacky sack, kicking a little beanbag to one another with practiced footwork. For some reason, one of the players was lying on the tiled floor. Beyond them, kids turned every which way in their desks, talking, playing cards, putting on make up. A propped up, spread out newspaper completely concealed the body and torso of the substitute teacher. No one really read a paper that way. This was willed blindness. The scene was less bedlam than a benign conspiracy. As long as the students didn't do anything truly bad, they could do whatever they wanted. I wondered if this would continue until the end of the year, or if the school would hire a real teacher.

Some hacky sack players noticed me, but appeared indifferent to the face pressed to the glass, so I continued to check out the room. The walls used to be white, but were covered with smudges. Thick cobwebs, worthy of a Halloween shop, draped the upper corners. I crooked my head sideways. The front wall was dominated by the chalkboard, the side walls by sports posters.

I'd been outside for a half hour, and the weather nipped at my face and hands. The sky remained sullen, stubbornly withholding rain. My stomach growled. I didn't relish fighting my way through a swarm of kids again, so before the bell rang, I walked around the library toward the back entrance of the stage. Fourth period I'd get a chance to talk to Becky Rivas.

To my surprise, the door into the green room was already unlocked. The tympanic membrane of my ear reverberated with the sound several seconds before my brain registered what it was. I was not alone. I went around the corner to the stage. Somewhere, someone was crying. The sound came from above me. High overhead, about thirty feet up, above the curtain line, ran a narrow balcony. Two pipe rails, one low and one about waist height, separated the platform from the plunge to the boards. The person blew his or her nose.

"Hello," I called.

"Oh, hi."

I recognized Amy Hirahara's voice.

"How'd you get up there?"

"Don't come up here," she said quickly.

I wondered if she planned to do something foolish. My gaze swept the stage for the way up.

"Really," she insisted, in a voice clogged from crying. "It's a little dangerous if you don't know what you're doing."

I took that as information rather than an insult. The girl

made her way down to the stage.

"What were you doing up there?" I asked dumbly, recovering from the adrenaline rush of the surprise and then the worry. Obviously, she'd been crying and had sought a private place to do it, which was exactly what I'd do.

"What are you doing down here?" She attempted a smile.

"I'm meeting with Ms. Rivas pretty soon," I said. "Were you thinking about yesterday afternoon?"

Amy's lips trembled, and her eyes teared. She fought hard for control. Thankfully, she didn't seize on the fact that I supposedly had not witnessed the baggage session. Probably I hadn't fooled her any more than I'd fooled Chendo. They both knew I was investigating.

"Public humiliation is the worst," I said, wishing she were taller so I didn't loom over her. I wondered if she bought her Levi's in the children's department.

A tear leaked down her delicate face. She impatiently swiped it with the heel of her hand. "That asshole Arturo."

The auditorium was completely empty, but standing on the wooden floor with the curtains open made one feel on stage. "What's the story with you and Goicovich?"

Her eyes widened. "What?"

"The cheating thing. The stuff Arturo was saying," I prompted, wondering what she thought I'd meant.

Amy led the way to the green room. "Don't tell Ms. Rivas I was on the catwalk, okay?"

This seemed to be a bargaining chip. "No problem."

She parked herself at a counter in front of a bank of mirrors. For makeup, I presumed. She stared glumly at her red eyes. "Only kids who have been trained, the technical crew, are supposed to be up there."

"I won't tell her. Cross my heart and hope to die."

Amy smiled, but I shivered.

CHAPTER 12

According to Amy, Mr. Goicovich had accused her of plagiarism on a term paper. Which he said was grounds for an F, even though she'd listed every source she'd used in her bibliography, so obviously she hadn't intended to pass off anyone else's ideas as her own. Amy sat before the mirrors in the green room and raged. If she was supposed to research a subject she didn't understand, she had to get her ideas from somewhere. She'd been writing reports since she was in fourth grade, and no one but Goicovich had ever demanded that she cite everything. As a matter of fact, she'd learned to write by copying how people did it in books, although of course she changed the words.

I listened carefully, not because I knew about the finer points of plagiarism, but because I wanted her to sense an attentive, sympathetic audience. By the time she took a brush from the drawer under the counter and worked on her long hair, I felt safe to say, "I met your friend Jennifer Padilla today."

"She's not my friend." Amy's hair shone and snapped with electricity as it sprayed down over her multicolored mohair sweater.

"I thought that you were best friends?"

"We used to be."

The volatility of teenaged lives stunned me. I made myself focus on the case at hand. I glanced at Amy in the mirror. "A kid in Mrs. Jameson's cooking class suggested Goicovich might be the father of Jennifer's baby."

Amy shook her head and quirked her lips as though she might laugh.

"Ridiculous?"

"He couldn't fit fatherhood on the itinerary of his ego trip," she snipped. "He wants to be Mr. Popularity. He wants you to think he cares. Goicovich annoyed Jennifer."

"In what way?"

Her eyes flicked up to me in the mirror. They hardened with suspicion. "Are you a narc?"

In my day, that term had been used in connection with undercover drug agents, but apparently the term had become more generalized. "Absolutely not," I said indignantly. "I just find all this fascinating."

"Well, you know Jenn accused Goicovich of harassing her?" Amy put away the hairbrush and inspected the tips of her hair. Since she was angry with Goicovich, and something had driven a wedge between her and Jennifer, Amy appeared ready to talk.

"Yeah?"

She tilted her face up toward me. "Well, he is the touchy-feely type, and Jenn didn't like it."

I sat on a stool so we would be on a more equal plane. "Touchy-feely like how?" My stomach quivered.

"Nothing most people care about. He'll say something, and then he'll place a hand on your arm or shoulder." She illustrated.

Even though Amy Hirahara didn't wear make-up, she polished her fingernails with a pearly pink and wore three rings on her left hand, which was so tiny that I couldn't feel it through the puffy nylon of my jacket.

"Some girls even like it. I know one girl who's always going to him with her problems. She wears these Lycra tops with her hooters hanging out. She's thrilled when Goicovich hugs her."

"But Jennifer didn't like it," I said, getting back to the point.

"Jenn said that even if Goicovich didn't mean it to feel sexual, that the girl I was telling you about did, and that Goicovich ought be grown up enough to sense that and send her somewhere else for counseling."

I was impressed again by the maturity of Jennifer Padilla's perceptions. "But Mrs. Jameson told me that you don't have counselors."

"We have one. And there's a nurse, and sometimes a psychologist."

"Did Jenn tell him to stop the touchy-feely business with her?" Jennifer may have been right about the teacher's relationship with the other student, but unless something had happened between Jenn and Goicovich, there wouldn't be much of a case. In my Cabrillo Criminal Justice class, we'd spent an entire day on this legal problem.

On the other hand, if Goicovich's actions made Jennifer uncomfortable, if they produced for her a "hostile working environment," and if she told him to stop and he didn't, Goicovich could be as well-intentioned as the Pope, and still be guilty of sexual harassment. For once guys really, truly, legally had to listen to what women said, and for some men that was a tough concept.

"Yeah," Amy said. "She told him. I was with her when she was working up the nerve."

Richard Goicovich better have a lawyer, I thought. "So if Goicovich isn't the father of her baby, any idea who is?"

"She won't tell me."

Was that part of the rift between the two girls?

"Speculation?"

"Someone like Arturo." She turned her face away from me.

Ah, so, I thought. A possible reason for Amy's tears and her parting of ways with Jennifer became clear. Arturo got to her because she had a crush on him.

"Why Arturo?" I asked gently.

"It'd have to be a major hunk. Jenn's sexually active, but she didn't sleep around."

"Wasn't she on birth control?"

"The pill," Amy confirmed. "And, not only that, she would have made Arturo use a condom. For STDs."

"STDs?"

She tilted her head and regarded me as though I might be mentally challenged. "Sexually transmitted diseases."

The feeling of pity was mutual. What a sad thing to come of age in a time where the commonness of the worry about herpes, gonorrhea and AIDS had given rise to a quick, convenient abbreviation. "If Jennifer's on the pill and would have had her partner use a condom, how in the world did she get pregnant?"

A blast of cold air turned us both from the counter. The door slammed behind Becky Rivas.

"Geez," I said, startled. "I didn't even hear the bell."

"Oh," Amy explained, "it doesn't ring in the new building. There are beeping sounds like a computer noise."

Becky Rivas stared at the two of us and did not look happy. Amy retrieved her enormous backpack from the floor near the entrance to what looked like a clean bathroom. "I can't miss honors physics," she explained, and flipped a hand in farewell to both of us.

With a weary sigh, Becky Rivas took the stool Amy had deserted, and plunked on the floor a woven bag, with at least as much stuff in it as Amy's pack.

"I can talk for about ten minutes. Then I have some kids coming and we have to start planning the props." Becky looked more like herself today, sans lipstick, and dressed in a black turtleneck, baggy blue cotton sweater and jeans, a woman ready to construct sets.

"I was just talking to Amy about the sexual harassment charge."

"Oh, I thought you were talking about Jennifer Padilla's pregnancy."

"One thing led to another."

"I see." She put both hands in her lap and fixed me with her gaze. "And what was Amy doing here?"

"I don't know."

"I see."

She saw that I was lying.

"So what do you want to know about Richard Goicovich?" Becky unpacked items from the bag. Sheets of paper, numerous sharpened pencils, a tape measure, and a hammer.

"Do you think he's guilty?"

"Indubitably."

"Why?"

"One time I was typing in the English Office, and Richard was working at the machine directly across from me. It was one of those times when we had to be dressed up, Open House, or some damn thing, so I had on nylons. Well, all of a sudden I felt this tickle up my calf. I slapped at it, thinking I must have a big spider on me, and it was Richard Goicovich's fingers."

"What did he do?"

"He grinned at me and said, 'Nice legs.'"

I scooted my stool a little nearer. "Did you do anything?"

"I was too startled."

"How about later?"

She put both hands in her denim lap. They were unadorned, wrinkled and worn, the hands of a hardworking, forty-something woman, older looking than her freckled face. Putting her hands in her lap seemed to be Becky Rivas's way of centering herself, as though she were about to begin a Zen meditation.

"I wussed out," she said. "I did all the classical things. I reminded myself of how helpful Richard was to me when I transferred up from grade school a few years ago. I told myself that it wasn't anything. That, in fact, Richard had been complimenting me."

"That doesn't sound like you." After all, Becky was a friend of my colleague Patsy, who'd led Queer Nation marches through the Capitola Mall. I didn't know if Becky had participated in that, but she'd protested the Santa Cruz County Beauty Contest and had marched in Take Back the Night.

"Richard knows I'm lesbian," she whispered.

I let that sink in. I thought about Chendo at the picnic table. This was not a community where one wanted to be thought gay, much less be gay. The hand up her leg had not been flirtation. It was a power move, as clearly as if Goicovich had backed Becky into a corner and groped her. "He's the only one who knows?"

She bit her lip and nodded. "Out here I'm strictly in-the-closet, Carol. Some of the drama kids may have guessed, just because we put in so many hours together and work so closely." She glanced nervously at the door. Watsonville was fourteen miles from our liberal university town of Santa Cruz, but light years away politically. "Watsonville High is a conservative place."

Not just Watsonville, but high schools everywhere, I thought. They existed to conserve society's knowledge, including its values. At my high school, nobody had recognized my brother Donald for who he was. And even after he'd come out as an adult, I'd been too shy to ask him when he'd realized his sexual orientation, who his first love had been, when he'd first had sex. Now he was dead. I felt like I'd never known my brother. "So how did Richard find out that you're lesbian?"

She moved forward on her seat. Her green eyes darted around again, and she said in a low voice, "I told him." Becky slid her chair closer, and nearly whispered in my ear. "He befriended me. I thought I could trust him," she said. "He has that effect on people."

That fit with the picture Amy had painted of Goicovich, setting himself up as a confidant.

"He even knows about when Shayla and I were trying to get pregnant."

CHAPTER 13

Viola Goicovich liked to talk about her program. "Some of the girls get pregnant to escape oppressive or abusive households. They think the guy will take care of them. Even when he does stick around, he's usually as bad as the family she left."

I concentrated on her words and tried not to burp. My conversation with Becky Rivas had been curtailed by the arrival of Chendo, Belinda and two other students. I'd departed to take care of my growling stomach. Now, Viola, a blur of color, swirled around a table, packing up birth control devices. One of my mother's aphorisms declared that there could be too much of a good thing. El Charrito had served its beef fajita bulging in a warm tortilla with fresh salsa. I'd devoured it in the plaza, happy that this time I didn't have an audience. The food had produced that bloated-stomach, nirvana-like stupor one feels after Thanksgiving dinner. If students felt like I did after lunch, Viola Goicovich was lucky that she didn't teach during fifth period.

The woman wiggled a neon green condom before my eyes and laughed. "Can you imagine this thing on? Be like making love with a pickle."

"Once kids are in your program, isn't it kind of late for birth control?" I asked.

"Never." She packed wicked looking IUDs, a diaphragm and a tube of spermicide into a white plastic case. "Some of my girls believe they're virgins. A lot of times I won't see them until they're three or four months along, because they won't admit they're having sex."

"Immaculate conceptions?"

She smiled. "In nearly every case." She tucked various packets of birth control pills into the case.

"It must make it tough, then, to get them to use birth control."

She nodded. The way Viola moved about the room, her size could hardly be from a sedentary lifestyle. "Norplant," she said, with the mysterious, clue-like tone of "Rosebud" in Citizen Kane. "Every girl in the program should have to get it."

"They don't learn from experience?"

"Nope. It's astounding how many of our teenaged mothers become teenaged mothers again. A few will have abortions, since they realize having someone to love is a hell of a lot of work. But for most of the Mexican girls, once they accept they are not virgins, babies increase their status. Purity to fertility."

"So it's unusual for a girl to give up her baby?"

Even with a body as round as Viola Goicovich's, a person can see stiffening. She snapped shut the case. "Highly unusual." No longer her voluble self, she swirled and put the case in a file drawer, then sat behind an old-fashioned oak desk that put a mile-wide barricade between us. She extracted a Pippin and a penknife from her desk drawer. Its blade was smaller than my pinky and yet appeared menacing. She chopped the apple into quarters. "What do you want?" She precisely and methodically cut away the core of each section. "Why were you talking to Jennifer this morning?"

This school would hardly win any congeniality awards. Everyone seemed suspicious and hostile. I could understand why Alvina Jameson hadn't hired an investigator, but I was beginning to feel like a patsy. I switched tacks. "Did you eat any of the cookies at the faculty meeting last week?"

She paused, quite aware that I'd changed the subject. Apparently hopeful that this bizarre question would lead to an explanation of my actions, she said, "Actually, no." Her plump hands gestured toward the apple segments like a game show hostess indicating the prizes. "This is lunch. I'm on a diet. The Forever Diet."

I thought of the greasy fajita juice that I'd licked from my hands. Life was not fair. Regardless of what I ate, I stayed one hundred thirty pounds. I told her what Alvina really wanted me to find out.

Viola Goicovich reacted like everyone else. She rolled her large, chocolate eyes. "Poor Alvina. She's such a nice person. No one is that mad at her. I mean, probably no one will eat her class's cookies again, but that's not the end of the world. Why doesn't she just accept it?" She took a bite of apple and chewed it lovingly, thoroughly. "So how does this connect to Jennifer?"

I had to think fast. I generalized. "Some of the kids from the cooking class, who are also in the play, seem to know what happened." I was thinking only of Chendo, but when I said the words, the hairs on the nape of my neck stood on end. Many people discounted intuition, but I trusted mine. It was not esoteric, but an animal instinct that preceded logic. There was a connection between *South Pacific* and the purgative cookies, I just didn't know what.

Whether from the injection to her blood sugar level or from my explanation, Viola relaxed, drawing a deep breath and dropping her shoulders. "You're right to talk to Jennifer. Even after she lost her part as Nellie, she volunteered to be house manager. If anyone would know stuff going on in drama, it's her."

She didn't say this as though it were a compliment. "It must be tough having her in your program."

To my surprise, a tear collected in the corner of one of the beautiful brown eyes. "If we could afford it, I'd resign. But the Catch 22 is with Richard's job up in the air, I've never been less in a position to quit. That girl has ruined our lives."

"There must be some other way to handle this problem."

"Of course there is," Voila spat. "Jennifer doesn't have to be in this program. It's optional, and Jennifer Padilla is too smart not to know that. She came to my program for some perverted reason. And we have a new principal. She doesn't know anything. I'm not sure she even realizes that I'm Richard Goicovich's wife."

"Who do you think the father is?"

"Not my husband!" She shot from the wooden chair with startling agility, the penknife grasped in her hand.

I jumped, knocking over my chair.

Viola Goicovich laughed, a bright infectious tinkling. "Did you think . . ." She couldn't stop laughing. Her eyes teared. "I was. . . ?" She folded the knife.

I didn't find the situation as hilarious as she did. I picked up my chair, but kept a wary eye on the woman. She may be laughing but seemed near hysteria.

With a knuckle, Viola wiped her tears. "Let's see. The baby's father." She plucked a blue tissue from the box on her desk and delicately blew her nose. "Maybe Javier Garcia."

"Javier!" What would Viola think if she knew Javier was the one who'd suggested her husband might be the father?

"Why not?" she asked.

Viola didn't reseat herself, which was fine with me. The adrenaline rush had left me antsy.

She paced the room, arranging chairs under tables. Desks weren't practical in a classroom for pregnant girls. "I guess you've met him," she added. "The guy is obsessed with Jennifer."

"He doesn't seem like her type."

"Jennifer doesn't have a type." The hatred had returned to Viola's voice. She gagged on *Jennifer* as though swallowing blood. "She's an experimenter."

"What about Arturo Arteaga?"

The whirling mosaic of Viola's skirt stopped. Viola tipped her luxurious blond curls one way and then the other, as though they were a scale, weighing the pros and cons. "Nah," she concluded. "Too regular. Jennifer likes the edge."

CHAPTER 14

I never had a chance to interview Richard Goicovich that day. After school, as I headed toward room sixty-four, an ambulance shrilled up Beach Street. Becky Rivas stood at the door into the green room, staring desperately at the vehicle.

"What happened?" I asked.

"I don't know, Carol." She was near tears. "It's horrible."

"A drama kid is hurt?"

"Dead, I think."

"Chendo?" I had visions of a suicide, his slit wrists bleeding on the stage.

Becky waved frantically at two young men, who leapt from the ambulance like dismounting white knights. The campus had cleared quickly after the final bell, and only a few students gazed curiously.

"Chendo?" Becky Rivas asked back, her smooth face wrinkled with worry and confusion. She turned into the green room and I followed. We went around the corner to the stage, where a group of silent teenagers circled a body. No one was attempting CPR.

"Did anyone check for a pulse?" I asked.

"I did," Becky murmured. The flatness of her tone told me that she hadn't found any.

Before the paramedics arrived, a student burst through the side door and flew up the stairs to the stage. A middle-aged woman carrying a two-way radio followed in at a swift, but calm, gait.

"Becky, what happened?" the stolid woman asked. I wondered if she'd been in the military, because her face remained impassive even as she took in Jennifer Padilla's body.

Becky bit her lip. She was so pale her freckles looked like moles. "The kids and I met in the green room as usual." She clutched my shoulder. "Then Amy came around to the stage and started saying, 'Oh my God.'"

Becky turned to the students for confirmation of her story. Chendo, Belinda, Arturo, Amy, and a dozen kids that I didn't know, all wordlessly bobbed their heads.

The circle split like a poppy pod to accommodate the paramedics. Jennifer Padilla's body lacked any visible wound, and her skin remained flushed, but she appeared unmistakably dead, lying on her back, her eyes open and staring at the beams high overhead. Her right hand bent rakishly back toward her forearm, suggesting a broken wrist, as though her last conscious act had been to stop a fall.

I glanced up to the catwalk and back to Jennifer. She had wet her jeans, a natural occurrence when muscles relaxed in death. The Yale sweatshirt made me want to cry. Here, before us on the dark wood rested a precious, promising life gone in an instant. *Two lives.* Jennifer's body, the shell, was gradually shutting down all systems, the baby too unformed to save.

"I just knew she was dead." Becky's voice tilted toward mania as she continued her explanation to the woman. From her air of authority, I deduced she must be the new principal, Ms. Salgado. "I called 911 and sent Zack to get you."

The paramedics didn't load Jennifer on the stretcher, but shook their heads. "My guess is internal injuries," one of them said. "Broken neck," he added, "but I'm not sure that killed her."

Using her radio, Ms. Salgado summoned Officer Azevedo to the scene. "And who's this?" she asked, inspecting me, but talking to Becky, whose grip was tugging my jacket down my arm.

"Carol Sabala, friend of a friend."

The woman nodded. If it weren't for her take-charge manner, she would have disappeared into the background with her brown skin, brown hair, and expensive-looking, but brown split skirt.

Officer Azevedo entered by the same door Ms. Salgado had. Although he must have been assigned to the campus, he wore a full uniform, weighed down with all the accouterments of law enforcement including gun, baton, and spray. He surveyed the scene and stroked his impressive gray handlebar mustache. "Dead?" he asked the paramedics.

"Yes, sir," one answered.

"How are the rest of you holding up?" Officer Azevedo's bushy gray eyebrows and kind eyes took the edge off his cop-issue body, six two and a solid two twenty.

Silent tears leaked down Amy Hirahara's face. Chendo had an arm around her and patted her shoulder over and over. The gesture seemed more like the nervous jiggling of his foot than anything that would comfort her. With a blank face, Belinda stood on Chendo's other side, clutching his sweatshirt. Chendo towered like a pillar of support between the two tiny girls.

"She was my best friend." Amy turned her face into Chendo's No Fear sweatshirt.

Death had apparently canceled their spat.

Zack appeared extremely pale, but he was Anglo, and a true blond. He remained slightly apart from the group of students, and I wondered if that had to do only with his late arrival. Arturo's body clenched, from jaw to fists. One girl whimpered, like an injured kitten. The entire congregation stared, transfixed, at the body, and Officer Azevedo's words barely penetrated the shocked reverie.

"I think Becky might need some help," I said. She'd gradually been putting more and more weight on me, until I realized that I was literally holding her up. Ms. Salgado helped me to lay Becky on the floor, and I cushioned her head with my jacket. The paramedics came over.

"Fainted," one of them said.

"She and Jennifer were really tight," Chendo murmured.

"All right, everybody," Officer Azevedo said in a way that commanded every head to turn to him. Even Ms. Salgado gave him her attention. "There are a couple of things that I need to make clear right now. What we have here is a sudden and unexpected death. It could be natural, but it could also be an accident, suicide or," he paused, "homicide."

He let that sink in. A natural death did not seem likely. Even with the complication of a pregnancy, how often did young, vibrant women like Jennifer simply collapse and die? The scene didn't have the staging of a suicide, either. No prepping, no note, no ritual, no dressing up or arrangement of her body. Plus just this morning, I'd witnessed Jennifer Padilla dancing around and singing. For all the tension of being in Mrs. Goicovich's class, her spirit was buoyant. Not depressed. Certainly not suicidal.

"The door to the catwalk was supposed to be locked," Ms. Salgado said. "Why was she up there?"

"When Jenn couldn't be the lead, she volunteered to be house manager," Belinda offered in a squeaky voice.

"But who let her up there?" Ms. Salgado persisted. "Surely she didn't have a key." The woman seemed more interested in fixing blame than in the dead girl. Her hard eyes peered down at Becky, who had the good sense to remain unconscious.

Officer Azevedo pivoted to the principal. "Why do you think the girl was on the catwalk?"

"Well, don't you think she fell?"

Officer Azevedo didn't respond.

This appeared to be the logical conclusion to me, too. However, as I craned my neck and squinted into the darkness, I realized no one could casually fall over the waist-high railing. I felt eyes on me. Amy peeked from the safety of Chendo's sweatshirt, pleading with me not to betray her, to remember my promise not to tell that she'd been on the catwalk that morning. Amy's self-concern caused a flare of indignation in me, a hot spark in the gut.

"I have to treat this as a crime scene," Officer Azevedo said patiently. "None of you are going to be able to leave for a while, except you, Maricela," he said to the principal. "I want you to contact the WPD for me."

Toward me Amy's lips silently formed the word, "Please."

I frowned at her. I wasn't a rat, but why was she so worried? Even if she'd left the door open, that seemed like a minor infraction when we had a death to consider—a possible murder. But maybe Amy wasn't being self-absorbed. Maybe she had something to hide.

CHAPTER 15

When Officer Azevedo's backup arrived, a detective interviewed us one at a time, starting with Amy because she'd found the body. He then jumped to the most inconsequential person—me. He took my name and vitals, asked me a couple of questions and let me go.

On the way home, I detoured up the grand hill to Archibald's to make arrangements for my baking demonstration in case school continued business as usual. I imagined it would. The lives of a couple of thousand people didn't halt because one died.

Eldon was filling in for me, which meant that he'd been at Archibald's since four that morning. He sat in the Employee's Dining Room drinking coffee. He didn't appear to be getting ready to go home, if Eldon had a home besides Archibald's.

"You sure must like Alvina Jameson," I said.

He glanced up from his creamy brew, half and half with coffee. If I knew Eldon, it had a couple of spoonfuls of sugar in it, too. The big man had hound-dog bags under his eyes.

"I sure do." He stopped. For Eldon, this was taciturn to the point of rudeness, signaling their relationship was none of my business. I saw the opportunity to escape without having to go through the bureaucratic maneuvering that passed for conversation with my boss. I got him to promise to mix an extra batch of reverse chocolate chip dough and to have it ready for me by seven, and I hurried out before he could switch from his smug, tight-lipped pose, to his normal, well-intentioned, but blathering self. And before I felt obliged to tell him about Jennifer Padilla's death.

At home Chad pulled his truck to the curb as I was climbing out of my rusty Ghia. He hopped from the pickup. The cloudy sky had blotted any sense of lengthening days and the imminent arrival of the spring equinox. The palm fronds rattled in the dark sky. I wished they'd sweep yesterday's niggling thought into my consciousness.

Lola rubbed my ankle and mewed piteously. Death makes life seem dear, and I scooped her up. "My poor, starving baby." In way of acknowledgment, she squealed to the neighbors that she was being tortured, twisted from my grasp, and leapt indignantly to the stone walk.

"Long day at school," Chad said, putting an arm around me and kissing my cheek.

Wait, I thought, until he finds out why.

The revelation was as bad as I thought it would be. I'd waited until we were settled on the Lola-shredded couch, Chad with a beer, and me with a mug of extra-strong decaf French Roast.

He did not like that I seemed to attract dead bodies. "This is two in two years. That's more than most people encounter in a lifetime."

Then there was the danger. "Maybe that girl was murdered. That means that there's a murderer on the campus." He swigged his beer and scowled at me. "Someone who killed a person you were talking to," he added ominously. This should convince a rational person to pick up the phone and cancel any obligations to Alvina Jameson.

He was right, but I still gave a speech worthy of a politician. If there was any imminent danger, the police would close down the school. Instead, about two thousand people would converge there tomorrow. Why should I be afraid if they weren't?

"You're as stubborn as Mary."

Any comparison of me to his mom was designed to piss me off, but I refused to be baited. I concurred. "According to my mom, I was stubborn even as a fetus."

"Well, Mary will be a stubborn corpse." He stuck a finger in the empty beer bottle and whacked his open hand with it. His lip practically protruded. Mary refused to stay in the hospital, but she was in no condition to take care of herself, which meant Chad ended up doing it. He felt sorry for himself, and resentful that his drama with Mary's cracked hip had been upstaged by my involvement with another death.

I couldn't, however, muster much sympathy for Chad. Mary was acting as she always had, but now the demand was big enough that Chad couldn't fail to feel it. The woman had collapsed right on top of his life.

This was my volleyball night, and I debated whether to go. Chad needed attention; I needed stress release. I couldn't do the former until I took care of the latter, so I went.

I drove Soquel Drive to Soquel Village and turned on Bay Street, only to remember the construction mess as one passed under the freeway. Gracious stands of eucalyptus had once hidden and buffered the on-ramps. But the overpass needed to be reinforced, and the greedy octopus of the Capitola Shopping Mall needed to widen and to extend its tentacles. Scarred mounds of earth rose to the freeway. Every tree was gone. Even in the dark, the earth looked raped. Californication was not limited to what our state had done to Oregon and Montana.

My brother Donald's memory leapt from the overpass and landed on my windshield. He had company this time—Jennifer Padilla. I sucked in my breath. The pain of Donald's memory was like a blow to the stomach, and I wondered if it would ever lessen. At the same time, I didn't want it to lessen. To lose the poignancy of his death would be like losing Donald all over again.

Somewhere in Watsonville a family was receiving the same painful blow. But for them it was completely unexpected. I bet that Maricela Salgado, the principal, was right. Jennifer Padilla's body had plummeted from the catwalk, whether by accident, intention, or with a quick push. I suspected the latter. For one thing, the drop from the catwalk to the stage was not far enough to reliably kill one's self. Jennifer was a Yale-bound student. If she'd set out to kill herself, she would have picked a smarter method.

I arrived at the middle school where the indoor volleyball class met. For an hour and a half the coach made us run, do push-ups and curl-ups, dig balls, practice our arm swings, and review blocking and defensive positions behind the block. The last twenty minutes he numbered us into six-person teams and we played.

I liked volleyball's balance. It required finesse in passing and setting, but allowed for aggressive athleticism in jumping, blocking and hitting. One worked as a team, but also competed.

A married couple played on the same side as I did. She was setting. He was the right, front hitter. The passer shanked the ball to the right. She chased. Her husband stepped forward to set even though she hadn't called for help. They collided. As is typical when one hundred eighty pounds meets one hundred and twenty, she landed on her butt. Life wasn't fair; he had been in the wrong.

He helped her up.

"You nut," she said teasingly, but with underlying anger, "the second ball always belongs to the setter."

Nut.

As I crouched into serve receipt position, I could barely focus on the round missile. The submerged thought that had been bugging me for the last two days burst into my consciousness, as though my brain were an old Commodore computer finally completing a search.

CHAPTER 16

"Reverse chocolate chip cookies," I explained to first period, "are chocolate dough with white chocolate bits." Outside the rain drummed. If March continued like this, I wondered whether the water would eventually wash the egg from the classroom windows.

Earlier Mrs. Jameson had read a special bulletin on "The sudden and tragic death of the much-beloved Jennifer Padilla." A crisis center had been set up in the conference room of the main building for students who needed to grieve.

Or confess, I'd thought.

The announcement had roused the class. They glanced anxiously from one to the other. "Jennifer Padilla?" they'd asked. "Did you know her?"

Their buzzes had constructed an identity. Good-looking. Senior. In drama. Pregnant. Ruben's sister. Uh, uh, they're halves. Different dads. They all have different dads. Live in that apartment above. . . . Eventually they'd filled in all the blanks they knew.

"How did she die, teacher?" the sweet Josephina had asked.

Alvina didn't know, and I wasn't telling.

I wasn't telling Alvina about last night's brainstorm, either. My suspicion about what had been added to the cookies had definite implications. I wanted to watch the movie of *South Pacific* before I made accusations. *Was I reluctant to deliver bad news, or was my procrastination more self-serving?* Once I solved Alvina's mystery, I didn't have a reason to be on campus, and I was hooked. I didn't believe that Jennifer had dropped dead.

She also had not seemed suicidal, but rather disconcertingly clear about her future. She was too competent to fall from the catwalk, even if she'd gotten dizzy from her pregnancy or had misjudged her body. A person would have to be leaning way out for a light or receive a boost to fall over the railing. No, someone had killed Jennifer Padilla. I wanted to find the villain.

During second period, I hurried toward the custodians' headquarters. There was nothing like pelting rain to drive kids to class. The concrete quad was deserted. I entered a narrow corridor. The fence around a swimming pool rose on one side and a building, an arm's span away, rose on the other. Drops pounded my head, and for the tenth time this March, I wished my black ski jacket had a hood. The sky was purple, and the alley dark. Beyond the wooden fence, splashes and kids' calls to one another suggested a swim class had begun. *Wouldn't a lightning flash make a stew of them all?* No thunder sounded, but I was still stunned a teacher would have students in a pool.

I peered into a dingy, low-slung building where a man towered to the ceiling. He had a full black beard and looked like a biker or bar bouncer, but was identifiable by the huge bundle of keys on his belt and the fact he was standing in the custodians' building, listening to messages on the answering machine. A nameless voice complained that the kids didn't have any toilet paper in the math-wing bathrooms. I didn't wait for an invitation to step out of the downpour.

Rasputin man turned to me. "That bathroom had paper in every stall last night," he growled, "but before school some kid decided to have fun and throw all the rolls in the toilets."

Alvina Jameson's voice came on. She reminded the giant that she'd called yesterday and that she needed soap.

"Everybody thinks his needs are most important."

The messages rolled on, punctuated by his angry comments. "There are only two daytime people for this entire campus." A red-plaid-flannel arm swung dramatically to indicate the vastness of his obligations. He didn't seem to care who I was. I provided an audience.

On the tape, Officer Azevedo identified himself. "Doug," he said, "it's okay to let people back in the Mello Center. We videotaped the scene last night. Nothing like an empty stage to make evidence collection easy."

That was the last message. "Me and Azevedo went to school together," the behemoth said. "Right here at Watsonville High. 'Course, things were really different then. We didn't have no murders. At first, I was going to be a cop, too, but crime depresses me. 'Course, since ninety percent of all violent crimes are committed by males ages fourteen to twenty-five, maybe working at a high school wasn't such a good idea. Are you a new teacher?" he asked. His chest cavity was so enormous that he didn't even draw a breath after this speech. He should have been an opera singer. He now gave me a thorough once over. "Did they give you the room with the leak in the ceiling?"

It took a while to dissuade him from handing me a bucket full of rags, but I finally asked if he remembered letting anyone into Alvina Jameson's room last week. He waved a dismissive paw at me. "Alvina should give it a rest," he said. "Nobody sneaked into her room. I checked with Al and he didn't let no one in either. Not only that, but I was in her room during her prep, because she complained about the soap last week running all over the counter. I thought I told her that someone punctured the dispensers. Stuck 'em with a nail, or something. I don't see any sense of putting soap in 'em if it's just going to drizzle all over the counter and make more work for someone. Do you?" He sighed wearily and tried to hand me a mop for the leaky room. "Alvina's been like that ever since high school. She's a nice lady and all, but a perfectionist. Always sure she's right. She should have married her boyfriend. We used to call them Spic and Span. 'Course now you say something like that, and someone would think it's racial. Probably get put on administrative leave."

I pushed the huge wooden handle back into his grasp and left before I was talked to death.

Back into the rain. The corridor was empty and dark. The fence opened. I spun around.

Darth Vader stood behind me. He held up a hammer.

Adrenaline pumped. Hair prickled. Muscles tensed. All my fight or flight mechanisms engaged.

"Oh, it's you," the figure said.

I was insulted and relieved. "Glad to see you, too." I grabbed my jacket's collar and tightened it around my neck to keep my shirt dry.

"Still minding other people's business?" Ed Smith tried to make it sound like a joke. He wore a long, black hooded slicker with a gold Wildcatz on the front, and could afford to be oblivious to the storm. He probably enjoyed watching water run off my nose like a spout.

"Is that your class?" I retaliated. Teachers were not supposed to leave their students unattended, especially, I would think, in a pool.

"Oh, yeah," he said with exaggerated casualness. "Just popped out to return this hammer to Doug."

"You make the kids swim in the rain?"

His chiseled lips stretched into a smile. The man had serious dimples, a weakness of mine. "Afraid they'll get wet?" he asked.

The rain penetrated my thick, braided hair, drizzled down my neck, and in spite of my chokehold on my collar, wet the top of my turtleneck. I did another of my *carpe diem* moves. "Hear about Jennifer Padilla?"

The dimples vanished. The gray eyes hardened to stone. Fingers tightened around the hammer. "Tragic accident," he mumbled.

Just as I was thinking how stupid I was to antagonize this man when we were alone in a dark alley and he had a hammer, a yellow blimp floated up to Ed.

"Heh, man." Doug's yellow poncho flowed and glistened.

Ed handed the custodian the hammer and, in spite of the torrent, the two exchanged a complicated, good-old-boy hand-shake. Doug pointed a sausage-sized finger at Coach Ed Smith and explained to me, "Another Watsonville High graduate."

CHAPTER 17

By third period, kids entered Alvina's room flushed and excited, talking about how someone had thrown Jennifer Padilla into the orchestra pit and broken her neck. Chendo and Belinda were not among them to usher the group nearer the truth.

Alvina considered the talk therapeutic, and I considered it potential information, so neither of us was in a hurry to get to reverse chocolate chip cookies.

The baby's dad was the hands-down favorite for culprit. But who was that?

My ears pricked up. I moved closer to a group clustered around Javier who remained magically dry in spite of the weather. *Was he the person who'd destroyed Alvina's soap dispensers? A job would do the kid good, but who would want to hire him?* I made a mental note to tell Alvina what the custodian had told me about her soap.

"The father is Goicovich." Javier's chest puffed under a pressed tee shirt. He surveyed his crowd with narrowed eyes, daring them to contradict him.

"That's not possible," a girl said from her seat.

"Why not?" Javier challenged. "Can't he get it up?" Followed quickly by, "And how would you know that, Paula?"

The stout, long-haired Paula flew from her chair, screamed ouch, rubbed her butt, and slugged Javier on the shoulder.

Javier tipped to the side, gripped his arm, and whimpered, "Oh, you hurt me, Paula. Maimed me. I'll never do another drive by."

"Stuuuu-pid."

Javier climbed onto his chair. Kids huddled around him, and Paula held forth. "Goicovich has a vasectomy."

"What's that?" a wide-eyed girl asked. Others shushed her. "How do you know?" an eager voice prodded.

"He told the whole class," Paula said. "He treated us to a blow-by-blow account when he was going through it. He likes to talk about sex stuff."

"What's a vasectomy?" the girl persisted.

"You get your balls snipped," Javier explained.

They suggested other father/murderers, names I didn't recognize until someone said, "What about Mr. Smith?"

Paula grinned wickedly up at me. "Look at Ms. Sabala. She's all interested."

I was leaning over the big girl's long hair, drooling for information. Fortunately, the antics of adults interest teenagers for only a nanosecond.

"You mean our P.E. teacher Mr. Smith?" asked the girl who didn't know the meaning of vasectomy. She had a distinct role. I'm-Miss-Naive-But-I'm-Eager-To-Be-Disabused.

"Naaaaa," a boy said sarcastically. "Aerosmith."

"No," Javier said, "Smith and Wesson."

Maybe it was Javier's line of thought that kept anyone from suggesting him as the father. Or, maybe Viola Goicovich had thrown out his name as a possibility to distract me from her husband. But why hadn't Viola simply said that he'd had a vasectomy? Perhaps because such a comment didn't deny hanky-panky, just impregnation. But then, the same was true of her exclamation that her husband wasn't the father.

Paula refocused the gossip. "Well, Mr. Smith does have that rep, and he kicked Jenn out of his class. A girl doesn't have to quit P.E. just because she's pregnant."

"I thought he was going out with the P.E. teacher over at E.A. Hall."

"Gonna get married. . . ."

"That'd be about the thousandth time."

"Yeah, like that makes a difference."

"Yeah," someone said, "maybe his girlfriend came over and killed Jennifer cuz she was chell-us."

These kids were as bad as I was, as cold-blooded, and as desirous of an answer. Maybe Chad was right. I wasn't normal. I was stuck in adolescence.

Chendo and Belinda entered quietly with a late pass. Chendo's jumpiness had transferred to an eye tic. In a touching show of deference, the other kids shut up, and returned to their seats. The silence filled the room with tension. Alvina assumed her stance. With her solemn, kind face, and gray slacks, gray wool vest, and white blouse, she offered a teacherly and reassuring presence.

I took the moment to glance at the green hall pass on her desk. It had been signed by Officer Azevedo.

After the class, I cornered Chendo.

"I have to get to honors physics," he said. His eye spasmed, the thick lashes tangled, and the lid flipped. He leaned against the stucco of the English Wing and pulled on the lashes to turn the lid.

"Your friend has been murdered." Rain crashed from the building's eaves and I had to talk loudly. "Your physics teacher will understand."

He murmured something.

"What?"

"They think Amy did it," he shouted.

"Why?"

"Her hair was on the body."

"But she found Jennifer. It could have fallen on the body then." Amy had also been on the catwalk where she may have shed hair. And, then she'd brushed her hair in the green room. Strands could have floated out to the stage.

He shrugged. Wet hair plastered his pale face. His eye twitched.

"Yesterday you wanted to tell me something," I said gently.

He shook his head.

"Maybe about betel nuts?"

He shook his head, but turned white.

"Like Bloody Mary chews in *South Pacific*?" I wished that I'd had a chance to watch the movie, to refresh my memory.

He shook his head.

"They're poisonous, you know."

"Jennifer wasn't poisoned." Chendo's voice stuck in his throat. I leaned close to hear him over the splashing water. "She fractured her seventh and eighth vertebrae, severed her spinal cord and exploded her spleen."

He sounded like a recording of an official report. He turned away from me, arm and face against the brown stucco. His upper back heaved. I heard only pouring rain, but Chendo was either sobbing or giving a Tony-winning performance.

CHAPTER 18

By refusing to budge, by acting as if I were about to become an adult appendage to his body, I persuaded Chendo to go to the Crisis Center.

Now I needed refuge from teenaged turbulence. I needed a friendly face, dry shelter, and food. I found everything back in Alvina Jameson's room.

"Would you like some soup?" Alvina removed a plastic container from the microwave. "It's canned," she apologized, as though bakers at upper-crusty restaurants like Archibald's lived on caviar and goose-liver pâté.

In response, I took a ceramic bowl from the cupboard and held it in imitation of Oliver Twist. We sat at a table, damp from sponge swirls.

Alvina spread a pink paper napkin across her gray lap. "It's been a week since the cookie incident," she said sadly, "and I'd still rather eat here during my prep than with my colleagues."

I didn't want to tell her that I thought the faculty cookies had been laced by a student—one of hers—with betel nut, a potentially lethal substance, if I remembered right. If I told her what I knew, she might decide my purpose had been served. I didn't even want to tell her that her soap dispensers had been vandalized.

"So you, and Ed Smith, and Richard Goicovich and Doug, the custodian, all went to Watsonville High?" I said instead.

She smiled, apparently as glad as I was to steer momentarily away from the "cookie incident" and the murder. "And Viola Goicovich and Officer Azevedo." She pushed toward me a torn loaf of Alfaro's French bread studded with pumpkin, poppy, sunflower and sesame seeds. Across the school's fields and over the zipping Riverside Drive, Alfaro's baked arguably the best bread in the county, even if a person included mine.

"That's just the group I went to school with," Alvina said. "Altogether about twenty Watsonville High graduates work here."

"Deep roots."

She raised her napkin and patted her lips. "We're a testament to how people don't change."

The Alfaro's fiber occupied my mouth.

"Doug was always handy, took lots of industrial arts. Richard was Mr. Popularity, played basketball and was King of Hearts. Ed was an incredible athlete, has all kinds of unbroken records here."

She excused herself, washed her bowl and the soup container, using a bottle of soap, and returned to the table with several plastic-wrapped Danishes. "I saved some of your goodies. Want one?"

I shook my head. "What about Viola? What was she like in high school?"

"A picture is worth a thousand words." Chewing a mouthful of Danish, she strode to her desk, ran a finger across books propped between wooden bookends, and returned with a 1970 *Manzanita*, the school's yearbook. She flipped to a section featuring the winter ball with a good-sized photo of Viola in a low-cut, full-length gown. She was stunning, not fat, but voluptuous like Marilyn Monroe, without the sex symbol's vacuousness. I didn't know how Richard Goicovich looked now, let alone in high school, but Viola's tuxedoed date bore a strong resemblance to Ed Smith. The caption confirmed my suspicion: Viola Costa dances with star wrestler Ed Smith.

"They were a hot item in high school," Alvina reminisced, her brown eyes dreamy with the opiate of nostalgia, her manicured fingernail resting obliviously by the photo. "Ed dumped Viola for Charlene, the woman who became his first wife."

Viola with Ed Smith was not the only surprise. As my eyes slid to the opposing page, I choked on my bread. In spite of shoulder length hair, ratted to a poof on top, and flipped out at the shoulders, I recognized Alvina, wearing pearls and a gown that looked velvety even in black and white. I also recognized her date, a big, fair-complected, boy Eldon.

"Oops." Alvina slammed the book shut on my hand. "Sorry." She blushed furiously. "I forgot about that picture."

"Who was Spic and who was Span?" I asked.

CHAPTER 19

The rain had slowed to a sprinkle. As I sloshed toward Viola Goicovich's Teenaged Mothers Program, I wondered why Eldon and Alvina would be so secretive about a relationship over twenty years in the past. Alvina had blushed and stammered but refused to comment. That mystified me, which meant I'd have to discover the reason.

I thought, too, about Viola's maiden name—Costa. She didn't look Portuguese, or, at least, my idea of Portuguese. It seemed everywhere I turned on this case, I ran into my own prejudices. How could I be miffed when people didn't recognize me as Mexican-American?

I climbed the steps to the dark brown portable and entered bedlam. Some girls bent over folded arms, some dabbed at their eyes with tissues, some wept in each other's arms. Some bawled, some sniffled, some cried silently. Granted, they all knew Jennifer, but the scene was weird, as though crying were contagious, or caused by their high-gear hormones.

With bare arms folded over a raspberry shell, Viola blocked my way into the sobbing derby. She presented a formidable barrier.

"You," she said, with even less welcome than Ed Smith had shown. "You have caused so much trouble."

My jacket dripped onto a scruffy, thin carpet.

"Look at this." She unfolded one arm to show me two short scratches. "Jennifer Padilla did that. I'd probably be in jail except Azevedo's known me most of his life. But, as he warned me, he's not the homicide investigator."

The pathologist must have found skin under Jennifer's nails, but why had Officer Azevedo tipped off Viola? I'd no sooner asked the question than I knew the answer. Azevedo was a Portuguese name, too, and the Portuguese community was tight-knit. They didn't come from mainland Portugal, but from the tiny islands of the Azores. The ones who weren't related by blood or marriage had families who knew each other for generations back in the old country. Of course, that didn't answer the question of how Officer Azevedo had known Viola was the one he needed to tip off. "You and Jennifer got in a fight?" I asked.

Viola snorted, and tossed her golden head, shaking balsa wood cows that dangled from her ears. "Only by the wildest stretch of the imagination. If I'd finally resorted to that, her body would be right here."

"She came to see you?"

"Right after you left."

"Yesterday?"

"Well, not today," Viola snapped.

That created a fairly specific time of death—from one-thirty to three-fifteen. But why in the world would Jennifer Padilla have come to see Viola?

"I was upset from talking to you." Viola's voice sounded rehearsed. "You got me focused all over again on how Jennifer was destroying our lives. I grabbed her arm. That's all. And when she pulled away, she did that."

"You just grabbed her arm? You didn't say anything?" I asked incredulously.

"I asked her to reconsider what she was doing. To withdraw the charges against Richard."

I bet you said that, I thought, but whatever Viola's exact words, the witness to them was dead.

"Azevedo told me the skin and Hirahara's hair were the only physical evidence." In spite of her desire to appear tough, Viola's voice quivered.

"How did he know it was your skin?"

"Stuff gets around fast."

The bell rang, and the pregnant girls stopped crying, pulled on their sweaters and jackets and left for lunch.

"Richard knows my story's true," Viola insisted. "I called him right after Jennifer and I got into it."

Viola could have received those scratches anywhere, including on a catwalk. A husband's corroboration didn't mean much.

I headed back across campus, checking the school schedule Alvina had given me. Viola Goicovich worked only in the morning.

It'd be no small feat to hurl a body over that rail. If Jennifer had struggled, her body should provide a lab full of skin and fibers. And how had the police analyzed the evidence so quickly? The hair may have been obvious, but the skin? Maybe Azevedo had simply told Viola about the crime scene, and she'd decided to come clean.

The lack of more physical evidence suggested that Jennifer had trusted her attacker. Had allowed him to get close. On the other hand, the obvious conclusion from the existing physical evidence could be the truth. Viola Goicovich had pushed Jennifer from the catwalk, and Jennifer had reached out to save herself, scratching the woman's arm. The woman had a motivation to kill Jennifer, the girth to force Jennifer over the rail, and a free period in the afternoon during which to do it.

The school occupied two city blocks. All I needed was Amy Hirahara's backpack, and I'd have a cardiovascular workout from walking here and there. I circled the main building and tried the door into the green room. Becky Rivas and the drama students had gathered there. Becky perched on the counter, trying to appear informal and in charge. Instead, she looked like an illustration for the word *stress*. Her skin was white, with the freckles popped into high relief. Bags puffed under her eyes. A wrinkled blue shirt damply clung to her body.

The kids sat in a circle on the floor, with a big, rustling bag of potato chips making the rounds. Most of the kids had sodas; one had a bottle of water. Several kids had candy bars, which other kids mooched, and the owners shared. Amy bit into a crispy red delicious apple. Zack had a fragrant, bulging, greasy bag from Burger King. He must have cut fourth period to procure it.

Becky looked at me. "We're trying to decide on an appropriate response. Whether the show goes on."

Zack stopped peeling tissue from a Whopper and waved an arm. "I think that we should still do the play but dedicate it to Jennifer."

The idea was received with head nodding that turned into a torrent of suggestions for the program. The meeting ended with Becky warning the kids to pick up every crumb or the City Arts Council would have their heads. They weren't supposed to eat in the Center, and she was in big enough trouble as it was. Rehearsals were canceled but would resume Friday.

Becky Rivas hopped from the counter. Her jeans looked as though they'd spent the night wadded in a clothes hamper. "Have you eaten?"

"Yeah."

"Me too." She sighed. "How about a walk along the levee?"

My hair was soaked. Water had penetrated to the core of the thick weave of braid. Once wet, my hair took a lot of drying. My discomfort couldn't get worse, so I said, "Sure."

When we stepped outside, Becky opened a big, pansy-patterned umbrella that she graciously shared although the drizzle had turned to a mist. She glanced at a black digital watch. "I can walk for a half hour."

We headed across and down Lincoln Street. An unmarked police car was parked near the portables. With its big antennas, it may as well have borne insignia. Becky tipped her umbrella toward the portables as we continued on Maple Street Extension, which bisected the hinterlands of the campus. "I'm glad that issue was resolved so easily," she said.

"Are you glad that the kids still want to do the play?"

Becky thought for a long moment. "Yes. Even with all the pressure I'm under. It would be too depressing if we didn't." We turned on Blackburn Street and followed it along the far edge of the campus.

"As house manager, did Jennifer have a key to go up to the catwalk?"

"Oh, no, none of the kids have keys to anything, especially not the catwalk."

"Chendo said that you and Jennifer were very close."

"Very. She was in drama all four years of high school." Becky's eyes teared. "Jennifer, of all people, understood the politics. The City Arts Council was squawking about liability issues before we even started production."

"I don't get it. Isn't that the school's auditorium?"

Becky gave a derisive laugh. "Have you seen the grand entrance to the main building? Our kids can't even enter the school that way. It's locked. Nor can they use the bathrooms in the lobby. The school has to schedule events in the Mello Center like any other organization, and, they want to charge us the same rates."

"They?"

"The City Arts Council. You see the City of Watsonville helped fund the construction of the building. This is the tradeoff, although they made all kinds of other prom-ises during the planning. Now they're afraid the kids will demolish their fine auditorium."

Given what the custodian had told me about the school's bath-rooms, The City Arts Council might have a point.

"They forget who the City of Watsonville is."

At the Buddhist Temple, we crossed the street and climbed a short flight of stairs to the levee. Brown water rushed below in Salsipuedes Creek.

"Amazing," Becky said, checking her watch. "For the last few years, it's usually been dry, just a gulch full of weeds and brush."

Across the creek, Watsonville gave way to pasture and

strawberry fields. We walked toward distant mountains, dark in the shadow of the clouds. "So don't you think your principal's right, that Jennifer must have fallen from the catwalk?"

"Yes."

"Well . . . ?"

"Well what, Carol? As I told Maricela and the investigator, I did not leave that door unlocked. We've been under a lot a pressure right from the beginning. This is the first high-school production in the Mello Center, and the Council is certain we'll destroy their facility. I've been super careful about who I let up there, and making sure the door was locked."

I debated telling her about Amy, but decided not to. This was not a woman who needed any more insinuations of carelessness. "Do you think Jennifer just fell?"

"Of course not. The guy from WPD who's been around campus is a homicide investigator." She emphasized homicide. "Sometimes he and Azevedo run out here on the levee. They're very buddy-buddy."

"Do you think Jennifer's death could have anything to do with her allegations of sexual harassment?"

She checked her watch and abruptly turned. "I not only can imagine Richard Goicovich shoving Jennifer from the catwalk, but also with his connections in this town, I can imagine him getting his hands on the necessary keys."

"You certainly don't like the man."

"I was sooooo glad that someone finally had the courage to make the sexual harassment charge. I was so proud of Jennifer and what she was doing."

"Goicovich must have done more than run his hand up your leg."

"Remember how I told you that he knew about me and Shayla trying to get pregnant?"

I nodded.

"At first I was glad for his interest. Glad to be out to a colleague. But it got ridiculous. He wanted to know every detail.

Where did we get the sperm? How much did it cost? Was it frozen? How did we 'do it?'"

I felt weird. So far, she hadn't mentioned any questions that I might not have posed myself. I wanted to know all those things.

"It got worse, comments about turkey basters and questions about did we include sex with the insemination. It was creepy, Carol."

We descended the steps off the levee. "It must be sad that neither of you got pregnant."

"Only Shayla was trying. I'm too old."

"Have you thought about adoption?"

"We've looked into it, but as a lesbian couple, we've never been too optimistic. You might think that being Mexican would help, but Mexicans don't give up their kids. Look at our Teenaged Mothers Program."

As we crossed Blackburn, back to the campus, Becky heaved a bone-weary sigh. "Yeah, Carol, it's sad for Shayla and me. Sadder than you will ever know."

CHAPTER 20

Life measured by bells. Even in my professional job, my creative soul regarded recipes as mere guidelines, so fifty-nine minutes of this, and sixty minutes of that, felt like Chinese water torture.

Alvina Jameson took time from her class to agree with me. "I'm so conditioned that when the bell rings, I have to go to the bathroom. If I don't make it because the line's too long, I forget about it until the next bell rings."

I hung my slick jacket on the back of a blue plastic chair. A bolt of brightly-colored, hibiscus-patterned material had been strewn the length of three tables. The students, all girls, were chattering, as one girl pulled tissue patterns from an envelope. Another girl had set up an ironing board by the egg-splattered windows. The windows were under eaves and the rain had managed only to smear them a little. Another girl shook a box of straight pins as though playing a tambourine.

"Belinda came over and told us that the show will go on," Alvina explained. "We're making outfits for Bloody Mary and her daughter and the dancers."

"Speaking of dancers. . . ."

"You're incorrigible." She glided over to supervise the ironing of the tissue patterns to avoid my questions about the photo of her and Eldon at the winter ball.

I plopped down at a vacant table and pulled folded, slightly damp notes from my hanging jacket. Drops of water fell from my braided hair. I made a mental note to drop by the drugstore to buy an umbrella on the way home. If I forgot, I'd wear my chef's hat around campus tomorrow. Anything was better than my soggy hair.

I'd just seen Viola Goicovich, so the fact that she was free this period didn't help. I couldn't meet the man, myth and legend Richard Goicovich until after school. I had most of fifth and all of sixth to kill, although, according to my notes, the charming Ed Smith had fifth period prep.

Alvina hovered over the girls who were pinning the pattern pieces to folded fabric. She gave me a warning shot as I approached. "Could you get me the address and phone number of a student?" I asked.

"Sure." Her forehead wrinkled, but she seemed relieved that I hadn't brought up Eldon. "Whose address do you want?"

"Jennifer Padilla's."

She gestured for me to follow her to the front of the room. I felt like a student about to be reprimanded. I wasn't far off the mark.

"Why do you want Jennifer Padilla's address?" she whispered harshly. She didn't wait for an answer. "I wanted you to find out what happened with the cookies, not to poke into this tragic accident."

"Accident? You think Jennifer's death was an accident?"

"Surely you don't believe the kids' stories about someone pushing her into the orchestra pit?"

"She landed on the stage. But that's closer to the truth than the idea of an accident."

Her rose-colored lips clamped together in anger.

"I was there, remember?"

"I have to talk to Eldon before I make a decision," she said. "This is not what I expected."

As I left, I wondered if she meant a decision about me, the murder, or the request for Jennifer's address. I felt a flutter at the idea "my case" would disappear, but then laughed aloud. I'd never had "a case." I was only snooping, and I could do that with or without Alvina's blessing. At this point, I doubted anything would stop me. I was, as my mother would be all too happy to point out, stubborn.

The mist had coalesced to a sprinkle strong enough to beat a gentle rhythm on the green, corrugated plastic over the corridor. It was the sound of a rain just getting primed. I passed three identical brown buildings that ran like barracks parallel to the street and the dirt area by the English Wing. Between the barracks-like buildings, strips of grass had been worn into patches by too many feet and too little care. I turned at the long business and math wing, which had a covered sidewalk in front of it. I stepped from the sheltered sidewalk and hurried across the open quad to the library.

The library was deserted except for two male students standing by the circulation desk. They both wore red, hooded sweatshirts, one with Bulls across the front, the other with UNLV. While UNLV stood for the University of Nevada, Las Vegas, the boy was not announcing his college ambitions. Gang members attached other meanings to the letters—*Unidos Norteños Locos Vatos*. Tough to translate: United North-allied Crazy Guys. The two boys also both wore brown, baggy Ben Davis pants. Mr. UNLV, whose knuckles said LOCO, was busy trying to separate the desk's pen from its chain.

"Don't let me stop you," I said.

"*Pendeja*," he muttered to his friend.

"*Tú eres pendejo.*" The Spanish got their attention. *Pendejo* literally meant pubic hair, but in slang translated to something like stupid jerk. They studied me, but couldn't see the Mexican in me any more than I could. My mom had referred to my dad as "that miserable man," and since I'd never liked him either, I had welcomed her attempts to obliterate him from our lives. Until lately. I was beginning to wish that I had a little more sense of my history. I pulled the pen from Mr. UNLV's hand and jabbed it back into its holder. "No one in his right mind would want one of those cheap pens. Do you want to look like you shop at K-mart? Why are you trying to take it?"

He shrugged. "Somethin' to do."

He was the bigger and more muscular of the two and reminded me of Javier. Doing something malicious out of boredom. They needed jobs. "Where's the librarian?"

"We don't have a librarian."

"How do you get help?"

Mr. UNLV jerked his thumb toward the copying room. "The woman who checks out books is in there. Fixing a paper jam."

"Are you here to check out books?" I asked. They didn't have any books in their hands.

"Pay fines," Mr. UNLV muttered. The other kid hadn't said a word. He lounged against the counter, waiting. He was the sidekick, along for the ride, which had as much potential for jail and death as Mr. UNLV's active destruction.

"How do I get help if I need to find something?" I asked.

UNLV shrugged and glanced at his cohort who pointed to the card catalog. "Maybe you could look in there," UNLV said.

"I don't think what I want would be listed. Do you know if the library has any of the school's yearbooks?"

The kid in the Bulls sweatshirt straightened and his face brightened. "Yeah. Over there." His voice hadn't changed yet. No wonder he didn't speak. He led me to the shelf. "They're old," he warned. "Back to the hippie days."

He sauntered back to his friend, shoulders and arms rolling, the gangster walk. But, he seemed taller, proud to show the way, to be useful.

CHAPTER 21

I headed toward the Watsonville High School gym to hunt down Ed Smith before the end of fifth period. The gym and the cafeteria had exteriors painted to match the main building, a soft peach with dark green trim, and offered no protection from the rain. Even though the gym had a ceramic-tiled roof and stucco exterior, the school was located on the central coast of California, not in the Southwest of the United States, so the peach and green struck me as more trendy than appropriate. The grand main entrance to the Mello Center, named for the local-boy-makes-good Senator Henry Mello, faced Beach and Lincoln, and the cafeteria and gym along Lincoln probably owed their face-lifts to the influence of the City Arts Council. A person driving to a cultural event at the Center and passing the school on Lincoln Street had the illusion of a rather nice, color-coordinated campus.

Both front doors of the gym were locked against stragglers to class. Country-western music drowned out my knocking.

Even standing outside in the damp, I admired the architecture. It spoke of a time when schools were built with an eye to beauty and a hand on the pulse rather than an eye on containment of students and a hand on the pocketbook. Through the glass in the doors, the interior glowed warmly with the richness of wood from floor to high rafters. The acoustics, however, were awful. The P.E. teacher shouted directions at his line dancers, and his voice bounced from the walls and ceiling. The interior swallowed the music and spit it out as tinny reverberations. A mass of kids, maybe fifty, occasionally stamped their feet, and even though they'd removed their shoes, the noise boomed. The chances of anyone noticing me were slim.

I circled to the back of the gym. A narrow passage ran between the pool's fence and the building. Under the clouds, the area was deserted and dark.

The back door to the gym, near the street, was locked. I moved into the dim corridor, mounted a short, steep set of steps and tried the next door. Locked, too. I banged on it. I could barely hear the country music on this side, so they weren't going to hear me.

I felt uneasy. My mind kicked into full-rationalization mode. This was a public school, broad daylight, such as it was, and hundreds of people were around, even if they weren't visible. Still fear rose in my gullet and turned my mouth to paste. I listened to instinct and beat a retreat toward the street, but a figure stepped from the swimming pool entrance. I saw red. Then something hard and cold slammed into my head. Blackness populated with blue stars swam before my eyes, and I sank to the wet concrete. The attacker kicked me in the ribs, and I curled up like a pill bug and passed out.

I don't know what humiliated me the most: being found lying helplessly on my back by a bunch of students, my jean's wetness from the concrete, the sense that I wasn't well-prepared to defend myself, or that Chad's dire warning of danger had been right. A whole group of students helped me to the nurse's office where I was dried, comforted, examined and patched. The nurse was a plump, efficient lady who told me that my rib was probably bruised, not cracked, so I was lucky.

I failed to see the glass half full. I didn't see anything lucky about being attacked and robbed. All my jacket pockets had been turned inside out, and my attacker had taken everything— money, car keys, my map of the school, and my notes.

The nurse told me that I was also fortunate to have my hair braided and up. It had made the wound easy to clean and dress. My assailant had broken the skin, and if my hair had been stuck in the blood, she might have needed to cut more of it.

After the nurse had me bandaged, Officer Azevedo led me to a closet-sized office.

"Feel okay?"

Dumb question. I gingerly touched the gauze.

He sat at a paper and tray-covered desk. There was just enough room for him, it, me, and the chair jammed next to mine.

"I'm embarrassed, and angry, but physically okay."

He played with his gray, handlebar mustache. "We've been seeing a lot of each other."

"Violent campus."

"Noooo," he said. "Watsonville High has an unjust reputation. Besides Jennifer, we haven't had a suspicious death here in a decade. Quite a few years ago, they found a body in an abandoned car on the edge of campus, and we had that drive-by down at the public library, but those were not school related. We have fights, some of them pretty serious, and we have theft, but these things are usually between students, and they're usually not combined. The fights are over girlfriends and boyfriends, gossip and mad dogging, and the thefts are usually non-violent, students stealing car stereos and backpacks, that kind of thing. Your situation is very unusual."

Was he warning or fishing? "Right now I'm concerned about how I'll get home." The thief had taken not only my car keys and driver's license, but also my Triple A card.

"I'll get Doug to check the nearest roofs."

"What?" I wasn't sure that I'd heard him right.

"I don't know why they do it, but the thieves take what they want and throw the rest up there."

I didn't feel hopeful. In spite of the flashes of red, I wasn't sure my assailant had been a student. The officer himself had just said the theft was atypical of student theft. Someone may have wanted my notes rather than the measly four dollars in my pocket. I shuddered from the chill of my damp jeans and hair. My house keys were on the ring, and the thief had my address.

CHAPTER 22

Walking toward room sixty-four, I longed for home and a hot bath, followed by hot chocolate with marshmallows. I imagined myself swaddled in throws with a hot pad on my lap. However, the best plan seemed to be for Chad to drive out with my spare car key. But Chad wasn't home yet. I had at least another wet, cold hour to spend in Watsonville.

The sky had turned as black purple as eggplant. Across East Beach Street the bottles at Martinelli's processing plant clacked. The smell of vinegar mixed with the fresh rain fragrance of earth and trees. My bruised rib ached with every breath. If I hadn't had on my fluffy jacket, I bet the kick would have cracked the rib, I thought glumly. Remembering the ignominy of waking up, a bunch of kids staring down at me, I felt my face flush in spite of a stiffening breeze that made the power lines sway. Worse than the growing egg on the back of my head, my aching side, and the humiliation, was the bullshit that I'd have to wade through to replace my credit card, spa card, driver's license, and library card. I'd worked myself into a lather by the time I reached room sixty-four.

Lights glowed dimly from the high windows. The door was unlocked. A man looked up from the desk. He had opened the thin drawer over his chair and was packing items into a cardboard box.

"Richard Goicovich, I presume."

He scraped back the wooden chair, rose, and extended a hand. "And you must be the infamous Carol Sabala."

He was not what I'd expected. Not a trace of slime. He

stood about six foot and had a powerful grip. The V from his shoulders to his waist under a gold Wildcatz sweatshirt testified to weight lifting. He had long, frizzy, almost red hair rubber-banded into a short ponytail. His mossy green eyes remained neutral. He seemed neither hostile, nor fawning. I liked him immediately, but I guess that was the idea if your life's ambition were to be Mr. Popularity.

He sat down and indicated the chair beside his desk. "What happened to you?"

I touched the patch on the back of my head. In spite of the nurse's look-on-the-bright-side attitude, she'd had to cut and shave hair to bandage the wound. That pissed me off, too. As a child my unmanageable chestnut hair had been the bane of my existence, but as an adult, it felt like my claim to beauty. "I was attacked."

"Here on campus?" He widened his eyes. His whole body was turned toward me and emanated sympathy.

"Yeah. Not that long ago in fact. During sixth period."

I scrutinized his face for a reaction, but all I noticed were the classical lines of his straight nose and square jaw.

"Cowards die many times before their deaths; the valiant never taste of death but once," he intoned. "Of all the wonders that I yet have heard, it seems to me most strange that men should fear; seeing that death, a necessary end, will come when it will come."

I sat, spellbound, crushed into the wooden chair by a mix of emotion. The recitation had been rich with feeling. I felt flattered. Unlike Chad who'd worry and fuss over my condition and think me foolhardy, Goicovich affirmed my lack of fear as valiant. He also managed to imply the thief, or thieves, were cowards.

"*Julius Caesar*." His eyes twinkled with enjoyment of literature, enjoyment of my company.

Oh, the charm and appeal of a man who is not only good-looking, but can quote Shakespeare. He attracted like a magnetic force. Yet, there was something contrived and self-congratulatory about the response, too, that turned attention from the cloying damp of my jeans, the pain in my side, the swelling contusion on my head, and back on him. And, what was all this talk of death?

He lifted a framed photo from the box, once filled with papayas. "My family." He passed it to me. "Those are my girls, Sarah and Jasmine," he said, beaming. "Gorgeous, huh?"

Two athletic, tall, strawberry blond girls of about twelve and ten grinned from the photo. They promised to develop into stunning beauties with model potential.

"They're smart, too." He paused and his voice dipped. "And you've met my wife Viola."

As colorful, graceful and pretty as Viola was, she was a blob among these dazzling creatures, a jellyfish among butterflies.

I returned the photo, and he put it in the box. He took a stack of birthday and thank you cards from his desk drawer, let them spill on the top, and extracted another handful. The top card was a sparkly, sentimental *To My Favorite Teacher*. "From my students. I can't bear to throw them away."

"Do some of the girls get crushes on you?"

"I'm forty-two years old." He excavated yet another handful of memorabilia, these yellow and dry with age. It was an impressive display, but then, he had been at the school for a long time.

"Girls can get crushes on guys of any age."

"I can't discuss the sexual harassment charge with you."

"Is there still a suit? What about the murder?"

"For this relief much thanks; 'tis bitter cold, and I am sick at heart." His eyes became sad pools of murky water. "*Hamlet.*"

"But Jennifer's death is a relief?"

"You are as persistent as Viola said."

I was willing to wager that "persistent" was not the word Viola had used. "She called you after I talked to her yesterday, right?"

"Right." He pulled out an old yearbook.

I leaned forward. *Did the drawer contain any supplies like red pens, or did it serve only as a trove of mementos?*

Closing the drawer before I could spy, he gathered the cards, threw them in the box, and interlocked the flaps. He set the box on the yearbook.

"She called you, upset, just before the murder."

His head shot up. "What are you implying? That I rushed over here and killed Jennifer Padilla?"

"You have a good motive."

"That," he said tightly, "is only slightly less ridiculous than the sexual harassment charge."

"And how ridiculous is that?"

Goicovich's skin tightened over his prominent cheekbones, but he maintained his composure. "I just said that I couldn't discuss the case." He lifted from the chair to take a wallet from the back pocket of his chinos. He handed me a business card. "My lawyer." He opened the bottom desk drawer and tossed a zippered, red, hooded sweatshirt on top of the papaya box.

I sucked in my breath, remembering the flash of red I'd seen as I was knocked to the ground.

"What's wrong?" he asked. In spite of how I must have irritated him, he was instant compassion.

"Is that yours?"

He glanced to where my eyes pointed.

"This?" He tweaked the red cotton as though a leper had discarded it. "It's been in the room all year. I thought I'd take it to lost and found."

CHAPTER 23

"Of course he's magnetic," Becky Rivas said over the phone. "Of course he's smooth. If he were some kind of repellent weirdo, he'd never get close enough to touch and feel and ask personal questions."

She had a point, but I didn't like her saying it as though it were obvious.

Chad leaned over the back of the couch. His wavy hair fell forward and his blue-green eyes glowered. While I'd taken a bath, he'd gone back out in the pouring rain in quest of marshmallows for my hot chocolate. He'd not only made me the hot brew, whipped and with a splash of vanilla, but also had warmed towels and my terry robe in the dryer. He'd kissed my boo-boos and ensconced me in throws on the couch. Now he stood behind me, drying my thick hair with a heated towel. The deliciousness of it made my eyes water. His actions were being underappreciated by my talking on the phone, but I couldn't help that it had rung.

"I didn't call to talk about him, anyway," Becky Rivas said. "How are you doing? I heard what happened."

Given the rumors after Jennifer's death, Becky could have heard anything. I downplayed my injuries and anger so that I could get off the phone and give Chad the satisfied mmmm's he deserved for driving to Watsonville to rescue me and then pampering me. However, the more I downplayed events for Becky, the more Chad leaned over the couch to scowl at me.

"I'd like to talk to Jennifer's mom," I said. "Could you give me her name and number or address?" The silence on the other end ticked a long time. The storm outside scraped branches against the windows. Rain pounded the roof. Chad had set up the kerosene lamp and a row of candles on the top of the entertainment center in case of a power failure. "Becky?"

"Don't you think that type of questioning should be left to the police?"

Chad leaned over and added, "Yes, Carol, don't you think that would be a good idea? Otherwise I'll have two invalids on my hand, you and Mary."

That did it. I was not about to have him lump me into the same category with Mary. I rolled my head and glared up at him. "I can get the address from Alvina," I bluffed to Becky. I wasn't at all sure that Alvina would help me, either.

"That would be better."

I thanked her for calling, sat the phone on the wood floor, and blazing with anger, turned to the home front. "Just stop it, Chad."

With a long face, Chad sat on the arm of the couch. His glumness was good since his dimples were an invincible weapon against me. The hurt in his eyes shielded him enough. "Stop what?" he said. "What did I do wrong?"

"You married me." I was three bubbles off plumb for autonomy. I liked pleasure well enough to sit while he spoiled me, but I wasn't about to listen to lectures.

"Miss Brick Head."

"That's the one," I said like Alex Trebek on Jeopardy, but my fingers sought the patch over the tender bump on my less-than-hard head.

Chad winced. He dropped to the edge of the couch, lifted my hand as though it were a fragile bird, and stroked it. "I'm sorry," he said.

Oh boy, I thought. This was worse than the verbal forays over the back of the couch. We weren't matched like peas in a pod, like Spic and Span; we were yin and yang, action and reaction. I'd guilt tripped him without even trying. "Wanna watch TV?"

He eyed me suspiciously. March meant March Madness. Basketball preempted everything. Basketball, to him, was a real sport, not like my volleyball. Chad never said anything against volleyball, but I could tell that in his heart of hearts, he considered it a wuss sport. On the other hand, I secretly considered basketball players, no matter how gorgeously coordinated, a bunch of genetic aberrations. A person seven feet tall couldn't fit in most cars. He couldn't even go to dinner without lifting up the table with his knees.

"What are you going to do?" Chad asked, not falling for my decoy. "Antagonize people until one of them shoots you?"

I stood and stooped for the phone. A pain shot through my ribs like I was being kicked again. "Only if they can shoot me over the phone."

"Who are you going to call?"

"Ghostbusters," I sang.

He didn't smile.

I sighed. "I need to call Eldon, to see what I can have for tomorrow."

His forlorn gaze trailed me. "I don't suppose it would do any good to tell you that given what happened, no one would expect you to show up tomorrow."

"I think that was the whole point," I muttered, jerking the phone line into the bedroom. Lola curled in the center of the quilt on the bed.

Now Chad sighed, loud enough to be heard over the wisteria lashing the sliding glass door. We had a redwood fence around our minuscule backyard, and didn't put up curtains. I stood for a moment, staring into the blackness, and listening to the howl of the wind and the rain blown against the door. In the distance, an electrical wire sparked and crackled as debris, probably a broken branch, hit it. Our lights blinked and went out. Chad thumped across the living room to light the kerosene lamp and candles, and in a minute he came in to light the candle he'd put on the bedside table. "Does the phone still work?"

I picked it up and let the dial tone buzz satisfactorily into the room. He stomped away in a funk.

I lay by my cat and stroked her comforting fur. Her head jerked up, but sank back down like a weighted balloon. She purred contentedly. In spite of the screech of vines on the glass, I felt like a noodle from the bath and hot chocolate. In the soft, flickering light, I wondered at Becky's reluctance to give me Jennifer's number. Finding out more about Jennifer might point to Goicovich as the murderer, and I had thought that Becky wanted to get Goicovich.

I popped up, startling Lola again. Her round green eyes peered curiously at me, and then at the waving flame on the candle. Neither was normal, but she was accustomed to my abnormality. She inspected the flame a moment longer, but decided it wasn't anything she needed to catch. I went to the bathroom, retrieved my damp pants from the hamper, and pulled the card of Goicovich's lawyer from the pocket. On its back, someone had written a phone number.

Chad sat cross-legged on the floor with his back against the couch. A newspaper rested in his lap, but he wasn't reading it. Light danced on the walls. He could have been engaged in a voodoo ritual. He looked odd. His back rigid. "Did you hear a funny noise?"

"Funny? The wisteria vines are rubbing against the sliding glass door."

"No," he said. "Listen."

I listened. I heard wind, scraping branches, rain pattering the windows, even the guttering of the candles.

Kathunk. We both startled. The sound, though, was the quite familiar twelve pounds of Lola hitting the wooden floor. She padded out, checked out our weird rite, stretched, yawned, and cried piteously for food. When neither of us responded, she strolled to the kitchen cabinet where her crunchies were kept, pawed opened the door a fraction of an inch, and let it bang shut. She repeated the process. Bang, bang, bang. Eventually the door sprang wide enough so that she could insert her head and throw it open.

"All she needs to learn is how to pour that ten-pound bag," Chad said.

I returned to the bedroom. Without Lola, the room felt spooky. Shadows snaked on the walls. I glanced at the door to the yard. My heart surged. Someone was there. I chided myself. Of course someone was there. My image reflected in the glass. I took deep breaths and considered my call to Eldon. If I reached him, he'd feel responsible for what had happened to me. It was one thing to send me in pursuit of a cookie tamperer, and quite another to have me mixed up in a murder, especially if he knew that I'd been assaulted. And, Alvina had probably talked to him. Not just about the assault, but also about the way I'd been sticking my nose into his and Alvina's private business. He'd try to persuade me not to continue my search. It would be better simply to show up at Archibald's tomorrow, expecting something to be prepped.

I inspected the number on the back of the lawyer's card and thought what the hell. I could always hang up. I dialed.

"Hirahara residence," a woman's voice said. It sounded adult, like Amy's mom, like a person who'd ask to know who was calling. I was stunned. "Sorry. Wrong number," I said.

Why the hell did Goicovich have Amy's number written on the back of his lawyer's card? Was Amy collaborating with the defense? Was Goicovich hitting on Amy? Weren't they involved in their own dispute about cheating? I knew one person I wanted to talk to tomorrow.

The vines scratched against the glass. I called Patsy, my colleague from the kitchen who knew Becky Rivas.

"Have no fear, a queer is here!" she sang into the phone. She didn't sound like a person sitting in the dark. Maybe the New Brighton Beach area had power. I pictured the tattooed pastry chef with her current Telly Savalas scalp gleaming under living room lights.

"This, unfortunately, is a straight person," I said.

"Rats." Patsy had recently broken up with her long-time partner, an immense, unpleasant woman who considered fat the only feminist issue. "What's up, Carol?"

Since Patsy worked in the mornings, she wouldn't have heard the gossip even if Eldon had heard about the assault on my person.

"I wondered if you'd give me the lowdown on Becky Rivas and her partner."

"What's it worth?"

"I'll introduce you to Donald's boyfriend's cousin."

"Oh boy. And I'll enter you in the Publishers Clearing House Sweepstakes."

"She's beautiful."

"I should ignore that politically incorrect, sexist comment, but what does she look like?"

I described her.

"What do you want to know?"

Chad peeked around the corner and made a time-out sign. "Just a sec."

"I heard it again, Carol. Someone's sneaking around our house."

It seemed crazy that anyone would be out in this storm, but someone did have my address, someone crazy enough to attack me in the middle of the day on a high school campus. "Baseball bat?" I suggested.

"I'll dig it out of the closet."

I returned to my conversation. "I want to know about Becky and Shayla's efforts to get pregnant." My ears pricked, and I strained my eyes to see past the reflection in the door. If someone hopped the fence, I reassured myself, I'd hear him. He'd be lucky if the wobbly fence didn't collapse.

"Whew," Patsy said. "I thought that you were going to ask me about something dark and personal. Their frustration with that issue is common knowledge."

Thuds and thunks from the closet diminished the possibility I'd hear any lurker jump the fence. I blew out the candle, so he couldn't see me any better than I could see him. My heartbeat picked up as though I'd downed an espresso. I was acting as though someone were out there. *The power of suggestion.*

"They tried a cryobank for years," Patsy explained.

"What's a cryobank?"

"A sperm bank. Tiny little vial costs about fifty dollars a pop. It's shipped in a Styrofoam container of dry ice. That's expensive, too. But at least the containers make good coolers."

Chad tapped the bat on the floor a few times, testing its solidity. Lola returned to the bedroom, and hopped up by my legs. Her purring instantly calmed me.

"Then there's the expense of the insemination itself, so each try cost them about two hundred and fifty dollars. Shayla even got pregnant and miscarried a few times before the doctor finally figured out there was a problem. Turns out Shayla has two uteruses."

I'd never heard of such a thing.

"Since they're lesbian, they didn't think they'd get past the home study for a state adoption, so last I heard, they were looking into private adoption. Very expensive." I was beginning to glimpse a possible reason Becky didn't want me to probe into Jennifer's background.

Like an apparition, Chad appeared in the doorway, dimly backlit by the candles in the living room. He'd put on his Nikes and a black nylon jacket. He gripped the baseball bat. "I'm going out to investigate."

If someone had come to terrorize me, he clearly didn't know about Chad. Usually I found his protectiveness unnecessary, if not a bit oppressive, but tonight I liked my fierce, strong, handsome guardian. He was committed to the idea that no harm should befall me, a trait that made us nearly incompatible, but now filled me with security. Any intruder had chosen the wrong house.

"What's going on over there?" Patsy asked.

"Our power's out. Chad thinks there's a prowler outside."

"In this weather?"

I ignored the comment. "Did you ever hear Becky or Shayla mention Jennifer Padilla?"

"Who's she?"

"Not queer, Patsy," I teased to distract her. My mind had taken an illogical detour. It was hard to concentrate on anything with my ears following Chad's footsteps, and my eyes flitting to the sliding glass door every few seconds. Patsy teased me back about having dialed Information, but I wasn't listening. What could any of this have to do with Jennifer's death? If Becky and Shayla had been potential adopters of a baby, maybe Jennifer's baby, that only gave them all the more reason to want her alive. So why would Becky try to keep this information a secret from me? Was her reluctance to provide Jennifer's address only a teacher guarding a student's privacy? "I understand Shayla's the one who wants a kid," I said.

"Becky wants what Shayla wants. Ever met Shayla?"

"I don't think so."

Outside Chad pounded his bat on something. From the direction of the noise, I guessed the palm tree. "All right, motherfucker!" he yelled. "You want to play, I'm ready."

"Statuesque. Talk about gorgeous."

Even though I could barely concentrate on the conversation, it was comforting to have someone on the other end of the line.

A blast crackled the glass door. I dove from the bed, pulling the phone onto the floor with me. Lola yowled. Outside steps ran, thunking from the back of the house. Chad screamed obscenities. Something smelled burnt. Lola meowed piteously. Patsy was calling through the phone, "Carol, Carol, you all right? What the hell is going on? Carol? Should I call the police? Answer me."

With one trembling hand I grabbed the receiver. With the other I reached for my cat. Cold, wet air tunneled into the dark room.

"Someone shot through the door." I was amazed at the calmness of my voice. "I'm okay." The hand reaching for Lola landed in a wet, sticky mess. "I think he hit Lola," I sobbed.

CHAPTER 24

The vet at the emergency hospital tried to reassure me that animals lived quite satisfactory lives without their tails. He was a tall, lean man in a medical jacket who didn't seem surprised that Lola had been shot. "You'd be amazed at how often cats are used for target practice."

It was a long night. The bad guy had gotten away. He'd been in a tree on the other side of the fence, giving him a big lead on Chad. Chad was now at home waiting for the cops.

The vet bobbed Lola's tail and kept her at the hospital to rehydrate her. Since I didn't have any children, all my maternal instinct landed on Lola. She was my baby and now she was missing the appendage with which she communicated: up and crooked to say hello, swishing to express irritation, or stretched taut behind her like a rip-curl flag to indicate high alert.

I suppose the person meant to shoot me, and maybe I should've been thankful he missed, but I wasn't. After I'd dealt with the immediate crisis and returned to my car, my eyes misted, but anger quickly steamed away any tears. I'd kill the son of a bitch who did this.

At home, the power had been restored, and I found two familiar cops in the bedroom with Chad. They were the same uniforms that had first responded to the murder at Archibald's two years ago.

"Doesn't Santa Cruz have any other cops?" I asked.

"We could ask the same about troublemakers," the taller officer said, putting away a camera.

I had the paranoid feeling none of the Santa Cruz Police Department liked me. Maybe they suspected that I'd helped the previous murderer get away. In spite of the justified dislike, the last remark had been unfair. I didn't make this trouble.

Chad shot me a quizzical look. "I guess you don't need introductions."

"I don't remember your names." Rain jackets with POLICE stenciled across them hid the nameplates on their uniforms.

"Officer Scofield," the shorter one said. His mouth had turned down, and the other features had followed suit. The unhappy middle-aged face spoke of a person disappointed by life and given to blame rather than change.

"Prince," the other barked with an air of arrogance, as though put out that I'd asked.

From the hallway Chad lugged a tarp and hammer and nails into the room, eager to cover the door. Glass spider-webbed for a couple of feet around a small hole. The four of us and the supplies barely left space to maneuver around the metal bed frame. The chill of the rainy night gusted into the room.

"You can cover it," Officer Prince said, "but don't replace the door tomorrow. We might need another look."

"Lola's okay," I announced to the group.

Prince held up a baggy, containing what appeared to be a small, molten piece of lead. "We recovered the bullet." He pointed at my once beautiful star quilt, now splattered with Lola's blood. "There's a hole in your blanket." Prince jiggled the baggy. "Looks like a thirty-eight. Maybe a Saturday night special. You can't hit a thing with those. Lucky if the damn thing doesn't blow up in your hand."

"The person either wasn't trying to kill you, or he's an idiot," Officer Scofield said, as though sorry my assailant weren't smarter.

"Is Detective Carman going out with Alexis?" I asked, both to needle them and to remind them that I did know people.

Chad tugged the tarp toward the door, swishing it impatiently past our legs.

Prince grinned. "Getting married in June."

The two police officers and I made our way, single file, from the cramped quarters so that Chad could cover the hole in the door. We sat in the living room where they asked many tiresome questions about what I'd been up to the last few days. I answered them honestly, while Officer Scofield took copious notes.

The next morning, I fit right in with the first period students. I could barely keep my eyes open. When they yawned at me, I yawned right back. After Officer Prince and Officer Scofield had left, I'd lain awake, hearing every creak.

Chad hadn't been able to tell the police much. He'd given chase in a pitch-black storm, no streetlights. The person had been tall, he thought, probably male, and had jumped into a light colored vehicle that could have been a Mazda or Honda or *one of those* sedans.

I sighed and inspected the students. I wished that I didn't suspect betel nuts had been the secret ingredient in the poisoned cookies, pointing a finger at someone involved with *South Pacific*. Would a kid go so far as to shoot at me so I wouldn't voice my suspicions? It didn't seem likely. The student could probably be expelled if anyone pushed the issue, but in the wake of Richard Goicovich's dismissal and Jennifer Padilla's murder, no one seemed interested in what had happened last week. Shooting at me would only get the kid in deeper trouble. Not that kids thought that clearly. Actually, the shooting would get anyone into deeper trouble, unless the person was already in the deepest trouble possible. Like murder. This shooting had to be connected to Jennifer's death. Apparently I was making someone nervous.

Neither the police officers nor Eldon had wanted me to return to Watsonville High, but the police had no legal way to forbid it. I reminded Eldon that we had an agreement.

He was in the bakery, up to his elbows in dough. "Not for a murder investigation."

He'd obviously heard the news.

"You know I'd do anything to go," I said simply.

Mournful eyes gazed down at me. Eldon looked just the way he had in high school, only fuller all over, as though someone had inflated him. "I suppose you would." His mouth twisted.

His brevity of speech was shocking. I felt ruthless. "I don't know the story of you and Alvina," I said to reassure him, in case he thought "anything" included blackmail.

From the dough, he extracted ungloved hands, which for Eldon was tantamount to being naked. "I'm sure you'll find out," he said sarcastically.

I didn't want my boss to feel this way about me, even if it were true. I appealed to his sympathy. "Someone shot my cat."

"This is your last day." He dismissively flicked his large fingers covered with globs of dough. "Take puff pastry."

So, here I was, first period, demonstrating the versatility of puff pastry. We used American Culinary Federation boxes of twenty sheets, but ordinary people could buy Pillsbury puff pastry in the frozen foods section.

I sliced a sheet of dough into four-inch squares. The kids clustered around, breathing like cattle.

"Mrs. Sabala, is it true you got attacked?" one asked.

People hadn't adapted to Ms. very well. Since my name was Sabala and I was married, Chad must be Mr. Sabala. To his irritation, about half his junk mail arrived addressed that way. Allowing people to assume Sabala was my married name avoided the tedious conversation about what kind of name that was, as the asker's eyes studied my Anglo appearance.

"Yeah. Someone stole all my stuff, too, cards, money, papers. If you see or hear anything, please tell me."

Given the sudden stillness, a person would think I'd asked them to line up and kiss my naked bum. Tell. They weren't about to snitch. I'd discovered a revolutionary way for teachers to quiet rowdy classes.

I continued my demonstration. "First, we'll make turnovers. The apple filling we make ourselves at Archibald's. It contains apples, cinnamon, sugar, raisins, and Myers's dark rum."

The mention of rum caused a stir.

"Don't get excited. The alcohol burns off when you cook it. It acts as a preservative, though."

After I'd dolloped apple filling in one square, folded it diagonally, and showed the kids how to crimp the edges, Alvina made sure that they all washed their hands with soap she'd bought, and the kids made their own turnovers. They were very creative about the openings in the top.

"With the square pieces, you can make strudels." I'd brought a blueberry filling for this. "The only change is that we'll roll the dough around the filling. When you put the strudel on the sheet, put the side where the puff pastry comes together on the top. You don't need to puncture the top because the pastry will pull apart a little as it bakes."

Again each kid made his own strudel. They seemed to be having a good time, and all thirty-two of them constructed strudels with only one dollop of blueberry landing on the floor.

"Does that hurt, teacher?" the sweet-hearted Josephina asked, pointing at the white gauze on the back of my head.

"Only if I touch it." The bruised rib was worse. It commanded all the other ribs, my whole torso, to act with it in pain. "Now our *coup de grâce*," I told the class.

"What are those?"

"It's a French expression. It means like a finishing touch." It also meant a deathblow. Our subconscious permeated every-thing—even puff pastries.

"We're going to make pinwheels." I showed the students how to take a square of puff pastry and make a small diagonal slit from each corner. They all did step one before we pro-ceeded. Alvina walked around offering individual assistance.

She could have sat and relaxed while I did my presentations, but she never did. I demonstrated folding diagonal cut to diagonal cut, crimping the pastry together at each fold.

The students were amazed at the four-pronged pinwheel shapes, and took to calling each other Chef This and Chef That with what they imagined to be French accents.

"Now," I said, "we'll put some cream cheese filling in the center, and *voila*."

CHAPTER 25

Alvina and I had exactly eight minutes to talk before second period started. Her full-skirted, red flannel dress swished around her knees as she moved about the room, picking up after the demo. The dress covered with a pattern of black irregular dots was cinched around her narrow waist. She'd put on darker lipstick to match the dress, and even though she had on short, black boots for the wet weather, overall she appeared less matronly and more like a woman in her forties who was still dialed in. She swung by her desk. "Eldon said to go ahead and give you this. He said that you're as single-minded as they come, and you'll get it one way or the other."

The piece of paper said "Lee Starling" and gave an address in Pajaro, a little town right across the river from Watsonville, but in Monterey County, rather than Santa Cruz County. The surname struck me because it was the same as the heroine's in my favorite book, *The Silence of the Lambs*.

"Jennifer Padilla's mother," Alvina explained. "There's no phone number on record."

Guilt stabbed into me again. Both Eldon and Alvina were kowtowing because they feared I would betray their secret. "You and Eldon don't have to worry. I'm not the type to blab." I wanted to give them both lessons on deceit. I hadn't really known anything. Alvina's influence with Eldon had started me wondering. Then there was that picture Alvina had not wanted me to see. The two of them together, the loosely fitted gown at the winter ball, a fullness to Alvina's cheeks in later pictures, the ones I'd seen in the library yearbooks—nothing really. They'd given themselves away with their reactions.

She shrugged as the first student entered for the next class. "It happens all the time anymore."

Did she mean getting pregnant? Or did she mean whatever had happened with the baby. Apparently, they hadn't kept it. Eldon didn't have any children.

Or, did he?

My next move was to talk to Amy Hirahara. Alvina didn't know what class she had second period, and she didn't have enough time left to get Amy's schedule for me since a phone call required a trip to the lounge.

"What would you do in an emergency if you needed a phone?" I asked.

"Don't get me going," Alvina said. She sank, like a bright streamer cut down after a party, into the wooden chair at her desk. I bet she had lots of regrets about what she'd set in motion by "hiring" me.

Kids trickled in, dripping.

Raining again! I didn't relish going back outside.

Alvina had posted a sign that said: *Kindly wipe your feet.* Most of the kids paused on the large, rubber-backed doormat to comply. They talked in English and Spanish, filling the drab room with life. In spite of Alvina's best efforts with bright posters, without the students, the room lacked cheer.

I took off so that Alvina could start her sewing class, although I had no clear idea where I'd go. I knew one person who might be available, but I'd lost my enthusiasm for prying into the past life of Eldon and Alvina. Still, the universe must have listened to my original intent, because as I left the protected covering of the corridor, I found myself alone in the wet outdoors with Doug, the custodian. He wore his nifty, billowing yellow poncho, so that he looked like a gigantic banana slug with a cartoon beard. He pushed a handcart loaded with boxes toward the English wing. I fell in step beside him.

"I'm sorry," he started, with no preface. "With this rain, the roofs are too slippery. I'm not going up there, and I'm not telling Al to go up there. So, we haven't been able to look for your stolen stuff."

"Oh, that's okay." I had forgotten about that detail, just as I'd forgotten to buy an umbrella. I didn't really expect to get anything back from the robbery. I just wanted to nail the son-of-a-bitch since at this point I suspected the robber had shot off Lola's tail, and probably was the same person who had killed Jennifer.

"Oh," Doug said, scratching an eyebrow.

I opened the door to the lounge for him, which further confused him.

"Well, how's your head?"

"I'll survive." Doug was a great source of information because he liked to talk, but the same quality might make it hard to direct the conversation.

He wheeled through the lounge, turned down a short corridor where faculty restrooms were located, and entered the English department office. The petite, bejeweled woman I'd seen before in the lounge and the copying room occupied one of about twenty desks. Books and papers proliferated on the desks, on a long row of file cabinets, on shelves. They stacked and spilled and spread everywhere.

"Hey, Hortencia," Doug said.

"Paper! Is that paper I see?"

If Hortencia had stood, she might have reached Doug's sternum. Doug made a comment about size that seemed like a well-worn greeting between the two. At her desk, Hortencia worked on a stack of binder paper surrounded by books even as Doug hovered. Hortencia's black eyes flitted toward me. She seemed to remember who I was, and to wonder what the hell I was doing there, but she was too busy to ask.

"It's not the size of the ship," Hortencia quipped to Doug, "but the motion of the ocean." She shot a sharp glance at me. "I sure hope you don't feel harassed by any of this."

"Not me." I didn't feel harassed, just impatient. Her exchange with Doug was automatic, like the handshake he'd given Ed Smith. Both reminded me of my outsider status.

Finally, Doug pushed the dolly on into a small anteroom. I lingered, breathing in the smell of musty books. "I didn't know you were an English teacher."

"ELD," Hortencia said, but noting my blank look, added, "English Language Development. Used to be ESL. Next year it'll be called something different so someone in the realm of officialdom can feel he's effecting change."

"Maybe we should blow up the works and start over with teachers paid in sacks of potatoes."

Hortencia's dark eyes examined me up and down, assessing whether I was being a smart ass. Was it possible that she hadn't heard about my notoriety? In the next room, the boxes whunked and slid across a gritty surface.

"So speaking of harassment, what do you think of the Goicovich case?"

She barked a laugh, and shook a short finger at me, the nails a bright, perfect red. Her bracelets tinkled. "I have no comment on Rich's guilt or innocence. All I know is that we're losing a good, hardworking teacher, and everybody's paranoid as hell." She folded her arms over an ample chest. "What kind of job security do we have if one kid's word can get us put on leave?"

"There must be evidence?"

"That's what some people say, but nobody knows of anything. Now the poor girl is dead. God knows what'll happen."

"If Goicovich really did something, would you still consider him a good teacher?"

"Did something? Like killed her? Of course not!" Hortencia tapped the papers with her green pen and thought for a long moment. "But otherwise, I don't think one mistake should cancel over twenty years of service.

People are so pissed about this sexual harassment thing and all the sorrow it's caused, they're going to throw the baby out with the bath water."

Throw the baby out with the bath water. A phrase my mother would use. Maybe someone had quite literally done this when he or she had killed Jennifer Padilla. I glanced about the room. "Which one is Goicovich's desk?"

She pointed at the next row, the far end. Unlike the one in his classroom, he hadn't cleared it. No papers were in evidence, but then the kids had a substitute who wasn't exactly making them produce anything. Most of his books were on a shelf that ran the length of the back of the desk. A couple of family photos sat on the desk, as well as one of Goicovich in nothing but bun huggers, his body oiled and painted with phony tan goop to better show his definition as he flexed into a body builder's pose.

"Good-looking guy, huh?" Hortenica said. She was watching me carefully.

Across the front of the shelf of books, Goicovich had taped senior photos of students. Amy Hirahara smiled at me, in a purple, off-the-shoulder, satiny dress, her long hair streaming behind her, the face a three-quarters view catching the fine molding of her cheekbone.

My fingers itched. I wanted that photo. I wanted to see if Amy had written anything on the back. Maybe she'd told him that he was a stupid jerk-off, and he'd posted it anyway, in a needy display of how loved he was.

Hortencia would not avert her eagle vision.

Doug came back through the room with the dolly, saying what a Mr. Nice Guy he was, that he'd not only unloaded the boxes, but out of the kindness of his *big* heart, had put all the reams of paper into the cupboard.

"There's a correspondence between the size of the heart and the size of other body parts," Hortencia said.

Doug's eyes gleamed. "I know."

"Hands, Doug," she said wryly. Then she did something strange. She followed Doug. They must have represented the tallest and the shortest person on campus. Their juxtaposition heightened the Mutt and Jeff appearance. Hortencia ducked into the restroom. The door had no sooner closed than I took a five-finger discount on the photo, shoved it into my jacket pocket, and tore after Doug.

"Whew," Doug said, "The Galloping Gourmet." The handcart clattered. "Did you set Alvina straight about those soap dispensers?"

His intent gaze ran up and down my body. Since I didn't want to nag him about finding my lost items, he obviously wondered what I did want. Hortencia had gotten him all lathered up, and he was a man of limited imagination in the first place. This could get sticky.

"Alvina is just the person I want to ask you about." Doug ambled, but he was so gigantic I had to stride, taking shuffle skips to keep up with the glistening yellow. "Back in high school," I puffed before he could say anything. Doug seemed so loyal to his alma mater and former classmates that I didn't expect him to volunteer information, but if he thought I already knew, he'd follow the law of inertia, and continue to talk. "The guy who got her pregnant is my boss."

He stopped in the quad. The rain meant nothing to him with his bright protection like one of Viola Goicovich's neon condoms.

A smile parted the black beard that sparkled with water drops. "Eldon? Mr. Span of Spic and Span. Well, how about that? Small world. I haven't seen Eldon since . . . the ten year reunion."

"Then it's true he got her pregnant?" I felt a little nauseous. I'd lost any incentive, any relish for unraveling this secret. I was acting on sheer compulsion, the sick part of me that made me bake up cookies even when I knew I'd spilled salt in the dough and they'd never taste right.

Doug's expression didn't help any. The smile dried, and his eyes crackled, so I thought again of Rasputin.

"That was the rumor, but you know how rumors are." He resumed walking, so that he talked over the rattle of the cart. "About fifty percent of them are started by malicious gossips with nothing better to do. The rest is gross exaggeration."

How, I wondered, could someone exaggerate a pregnancy? It was like the old joke. A person couldn't be a little pregnant. "Did she ever have a baby?"

"No," he said curtly, "she didn't."

He reached the corridor to the janitor's shed. Even though we were not at the end of the pool where I'd been attacked, the narrow dimness made my hairs prickle. "They seem like such a perfect couple. I wonder why they didn't just get married and have the kid."

Doug paused before his shed and used a key on his enormous ring to unlock it. He puffed up even bigger, like some sort of mating fish, as though my following him to his domain confirmed that I had designs on his body. He parked the cart in the dark interior and pulled off his yellow slicker. He hung the dripping plastic on a wall peg, and towered above me, dark and ominous. The shed provided little head clearance for him. "They had places to go and things to do."

I'd been playing devil's advocate to some degree, and I liked the fact that Doug defended Eldon and Alvina and supported their decision, but I also wondered how far loyalty to school peers would take him.

"Are you in charge of the keys for this school, Doug?"

In response, he stretched the huge bundle of keys from his belt, unlocked a side door, drew back two deadbolts, and showed me a windowless, closet-sized room, containing nothing but a counter, a key grinder, and peg boards covered with numbered keys.

"So you know who has what keys."

He guffawed bitterly. "Fat chance. The staff here is so bad

about turning in their keys for the summer that I haven't had an accurate inventory since about 1980. That's what I told the cops, too."

The way he said it, I didn't think he meant his friend Officer Azevedo.

"You sure are a spunky gal," he said. "Most people would have quit snooping around after what happened yesterday."

I thought of the shooting. He didn't know the half of it. Or, did he? "Well, I'm not normal. Just ask my husband."

Doug glanced at my ringless left hand. My wedding ring was an ornate fixture of one large and two small rubies, from which I'd have to pick dough with a straight pin if I wore it while preparing pastries. I didn't feel like explaining this to Doug. The message ought to be clear whether he believed I was married or not.

"Of course, as I also told the cops," he moved closer as though he liked hard-to-get and viewed my statement as a challenge, "the new building being new, it's a little different story."

Doug now stood a fraction too close. Men and women certainly did understand things differently. At least, Doug and I did. No wonder sexual harassment charges were rife. "So you know who has keys to the Mello Center?"

"Exactamundo. Me and Al. Ms. Salgado, that's the new principal. Becky Rivas, the drama teacher, and two keys to the City Arts Council."

"So, Doug." He seemed to like spunk. I leaned toward him, neck tilted back, and smiled. It felt whorish, but it was a great way to get information, a tradeoff for the inequality in size and strength. My mom always said you got more flies with honey than vinegar, to which I'd saucily replied, "Gawd, ma, who wants more flies." But in my new line of work, one wanted not only to attract, but also to capture, flies.

In response to my flirty voice, Doug tugged his full black beard.

"Who's in charge of this City Arts Council?"

"What's it worth?"

A fat lip. "I'll let you see my hair down." I lifted an eyebrow, one of my great talents.

The colossus leered, masturbating his facial hair, apparently reading the entire Kama Sutra into the remark. "Rose Scurich has one. She's president. And Charlene Hankemeier, the secretary, has the other. Charlene was Ed Smith's first wife." He shrugged his shoulders. "His best wife."

I pivoted before Doug asked for the specifics of our supposed rendezvous. He reached for my arm, but was too late. I scrammed out the door into the drizzle.

CHAPTER 26

I killed the rest of second period in the deserted library. What a shame for it not to be used. The round building was pleasant, a trifle overheated, and full of the fusty scent of books. It had windows all the way around, although side rooms, like that for the copying machine, obstructed the view. I guessed, though, that a library without a librarian was a bit like a car without an engine.

Alone and out of the rain, I pulled the senior class photograph of Amy from my pocket and flipped it over. She'd written to Goicovich: "We'll see. Amy." *Cryptic*. We'll see about what? I had to talk to that girl. I inspected the pretty, flawless face on the front. Richard Goicovich couldn't find a female more opposite in appearance to his wife—tiny and dark with a degree of Japanese reserve. At least I knew the class Amy had during fourth period. The library clerk emerged from the copy machine room, and I approached her at the circulation desk. "Could you tell me the room for honors physics?"

"No," she said. She was an unsmiling woman. I was ready to leave when she decided to grace me by saying, "Mr. Conners teaches that. There's a schedule of teachers by the office phone." She aimed a knobby finger at the target.

I gave her my most sincere thank you so maybe next time she'd be more forthcoming. I spent the rest of the period looking at the old yearbooks, finding pictures of the people I'd met here, feeling melancholy down to my toes. I wondered if Eldon and Alvina regretted having an abortion. Or, maybe Alvina had miscarried. Either way, they'd ended up with careers, but both seemed to be unmarried and without children. The students called Alvina Mrs. Jameson, but that didn't mean anything. They still addressed me as Mrs. after I'd explained about Ms.

Even as a person who didn't plan to have children, I found Eldon and Alvina's situation sad. Under Eldon's long hours at work, I sensed loneliness. Why go home? There was nothing to go home to. And I knew from Eldon's crush on a friend of mine that he wasn't impervious to the idea of a relationship. Why hadn't he and Alvina gotten together later? Had the miscarriage or abortion changed their feelings forever?

Without wiping his feet, Javier swaggered into Alvina's room, came up to me with his massive shoulders rolling under his red sweatshirt, and said, "Hear you got jumped." He smiled without sympathy. I stared at his backwards red cap, remembering the flash of red when I was attacked. Maybe a hoodlum *had* robbed me, and the assault had nothing to do with my investigation.

"So did you have a good time with that four dollars?" I was grabbing at straws, scrutinizing his face for a telltale sign.

"Say what?" His expression shifted from convincing blank to dawning indignation. His mouth fell open.

"You seem to enjoy the fact I was beaten and robbed."

His eyes widened and his face drew back as though slapped. He had the sense to look contrite. For a moment. He swiped off his cap. "I didn't do it."

"Do you know who did?"

He slapped his brown baggies a couple of times with his hat and glared at me, the indignation coalescing. "You're accusing me because I'm Mexican." He pronounced this loudly, so that dark eyes all around the room turned toward us. He lifted his chin. Paula aggressively strutted over, ready to defend *la raza*.

If I weren't so livid, I would have laughed. I didn't feel like digressing about my surname Sabala. To them, I wasn't even a coconut, brown on the outside and white on the inside. I was assimilated and appeared white, ergo I was white. "Javier, nearly this whole class is Mexican." I made a sweeping gesture around the room.

"What's wrong with that?" Paula interjected.

I kept my eyes fixed on Javier's. "I'd guess about eighty percent of your school is Mexican, and I'm not suggesting any of them were involved. Just you."

"You're judging me because of the way I dress."

"Yeah," Paula said.

"And the way you act."

He straightened and jammed his hat on his thick, dark hair. "What did I supposedly do?"

"For one thing, you punctured Ms. Jameson's soap dispensers." I was taking a stab in the dark, but it hit home and caught Javier off guard. He'd expected me to accuse him of the theft of my stuff. His denial came a second too late. Paula studied him with big eyes, then walked swiftly toward the sinks. She'd see for herself. Suddenly Javier was not so interested in being loud and aggressive. I glimpsed, as I had in the plaza, the fifteen-year-old.

"I'll make you a deal," I said.

His eyes narrowed. He removed his cap again and skimmed a hand along his brushed back hair.

"I'll still ask my boss about a job for you, but you'll have to do something to pay for the damage you did to the dispensers."

The bell rang and kids took their seats. Javier and I edged over to the far side of the room, near the dirty windows. Alvina could sense that we were in the middle of something important. She told various kids to get the fillings and puff pastry for my demo and set others to work gathering items.

"You can't prove I did that," Javier said.

"No, I can't. But I know you did."

"You don't have no evidence."

"True."

He didn't walk away. "So what do I have to do?"

"Clean the egg off these windows."

"I didn't throw no eggs!"

In unison, the class wheeled to stare. I didn't say anything. After waiting a minute for the drama to continue, the students got bored and turned back to the business of arranging the room for the demonstration.

"I didn't say you did, Javier."

"Then why should I have to clean the windows?"

"Reparations."

"Huh?"

"Look, Javier, if I'm going to be your advocate, I have to know that you can be responsible. Responsible people pay for their mistakes."

"But I didn't do the windows. I swear."

"I know. But you did ruin the soap dispensers."

"But I don't want to work outside."

I understood. It wasn't because of the rain. If he was outside, people could see him. His macho pride was at stake. "I don't care what you want, Javier." Actually, I did care, but not about his whiny immediate desires, but rather his aspirations and dreams, and he'd never reach those by indulging his whims. "That's the deal."

He turned abruptly and sauntered, exaggerating the gorilla arm swing of a gangsta, to the group of kids in front of the table.

I felt somewhat successful. He hadn't told me that he wouldn't clean no windows.

CHAPTER 27

I didn't need to consult a map to find the room for honors physics, a good thing since mine had been stolen. Chendo had that class. All I had to do was follow him. Still anger bubbled up at all the inconvenience the thief had caused me. He was probably the shooter, too. That thought made me livid.

Chendo lagged in Alvina Jameson's room, tying his shoes. "Go ahead," he told Belinda. All the other students had left. Chendo untied his other athletic shoe and cinched the wet laces tighter. At this rate, I'd never intercept Amy. She'd arrive at honors physics and become inextricably busy figuring out how to pack an egg so that it could be dropped without breaking from a two-story building. Or whatever it was they did in honors physics.

I stepped outside and studied the room numbers to get a sense of which way they ran. Rain pattered against the green plastic over my head. Chendo followed me out, but instead of leading my way to honors physics, he stopped a few feet from me. "Is everything okay, Chendo?"

"I heard you talking to Javier."

"Yes." I was glad that I wasn't a mother, because eventually a sweet little baby would become a teenager. As a matter of fact, he'd be a teenager longer than he was a baby, toddler and child combined. And I simply didn't have the patience for these elliptical teenage approaches to every subject.

The long-lashed eyes scanned the eaves of the barracks-like buildings. Water gurgled from the drains, but the rain had stopped. "Do you think the police will arrest the person who messed up the cookies?"

"With Jennifer's murder and my assault, people have practically forgotten the cookies. They wish Ms. Jameson would forget the cookies, too." Revelation hovered in the damp air. I listened to the ticking and trickling of the water, but Chendo wasn't quite ready, so I talked on, "No one was seriously hurt, and no one is pressing charges, especially not Ms. Jameson. In another week, people will be joking about The Great Puke Fest."

"What reparation do you think that person should make?"

"I think that he should help me get Amy Hirahara out of honors physics."

He widened his eyes, but seemed otherwise unastonished that I knew. "That's all?"

Did his histrionic heart demand a public flogging?

"Oh, eventually, he should tell Ms. Jameson what happened, but I'd appreciate it if he waited 'til next week." In his nervous guilt, I saw something beyond simply "not cool." Chendo was like a van Gogh painting--sensitive, great to look at, very bright, and not quite right. "Why did you do it?"

He shrugged in a way that reminded me of Javier when I asked about turning up the ovens. Confusion, not apathy. They really did not understand their own actions.

"In the movie, Bloody Mary looks all happy," he said lamely. "I just wanted the teachers . . . the school . . . to feel that way again. I thought betel nut was like an upper. She chews it all the time in the movie."

I held my breath to restrain a lecture. Betel nut contained a poisonous alkaloid, a five on a scale of six for toxicity. He could have killed someone. But he hadn't, and I doubted he'd try another stunt like that one.

Chendo extracted his arms from a blue backpack, rolled a pen from a pouch, and turned to face the stucco wall. He took a note pad, the size of Post-Its, from a pocket of his jeans.

"What are those?"

"Office passes."

These were surely contraband, but since I wasn't telling about the cookies, he'd decided to trust me.

"Won't your teacher be suspicious?"

"Mr. Conners?" For sheer stupidity, my question apparently ranked with leaping from an airplane without a parachute.

"How does he maintain control of the class?" I asked, thinking of Richard Goicovich's substitute.

"That class is so hard, if you even blink, you won't know what's going on."

"So maybe Amy will ignore the pass."

"I'll sign it Officer Azevedo." He tore off the pass, and put the rest back in his pocket. "You just wait outside the room for Amy."

He shrugged his pack on over his sweatshirt and walked a short distance to the science room.

I trotted behind him. "Chendo, how did you get your hands on betel nuts?"

"A chat room."

He slipped into the classroom. I waited off to the side of the door. The tardy bell rang. So Chendo had "met" someone with access to betel nuts, and had persuaded the person, possibly a kid, to send him some.

From the high, open windows drifted the soft, but authoritative voice of Mr. Conners telling Amy she had a call slip, Amy's wheedling protest, and Mr. Conners' insistence.

Free of her pack, Amy flounced from the room, hair flying behind her black, cotton sweat suit. She pushed at the door so that it would slam, but the pneumatic hinge impeded the dramatic exit. She immediately sensed my presence and whirled. "What are you doing here?" Her smooth forehead managed a single wrinkle.

I sprang toward the quad to lure Amy away from the open windows. "Where do you have to go?"

"Officer Azevedo." She fell in step beside me, staying on the walk by the business wing to avoid the block of mud in front of the English classrooms. If she had a jacket, she'd left it in the classroom. A person couldn't leave in a proper huff if she stopped to don clothing. "Shit."

"What's the matter?"

"Just shit."

I stopped in the middle of the quad, pocked with empty squares awaiting trees.

Amy stopped, too. "I don't mean to be cold about Jenn's death, but I can *not* afford to miss physics. I'm barely getting a C."

"Isn't a C in honors the same as a B?"

"Yeah."

"Haven't students already applied to and been accepted or rejected from colleges?"

"Sure. I'm going to Cal." She grinned. "But that doesn't change my parents' expectations."

"Seems like you'd be more worried about a possible F in English."

"A D," she said flatly. She averted her eyes, but nodded. "Of course I'm worried about that." A soap opera actress could have done a better job with the lines.

"That fourth year of English is required, isn't it?" It had been back in my day.

"Yes."

"Does the University of California accept a D?"

"No."

"Well, Berkeley, geez. I'd think you'd need almost perfect grades. Maybe one of the other UC's would let you in."

Her scowl said I had the mind of an earthworm. "I'm not exactly an underrepresented minority."

"Which is why I think you should be sweating bullets over a D in English."

"I've gotta go."

"No, you don't. I had Chendo write that pass."

"Why? Shit. Are you trying to ruin my future?" She slammed a tiny fist against her thigh. "Shit, double shit." She shook her head to avoid tears. "What do you want?"

"Your phone number is on the back of a business card Mr. Goicovich got from his lawyer. And gave me. Accidentally, I'm sure."

"So?" she retorted, but her face blanched.

"So why's he calling you?"

"He probably called my mom about the so-called cheating."

"Probably, Amy?"

The girl shivered from the damp chill. Or fear. Her compact body drooped as though soggy from the moisture in the air.

"From the way you've described your parents," I continued, "if your mother received a phone call from Mr. Goicovich, you'd know."

"Maybe he didn't get around to it. Who are you anyway?" She took a step back toward the science wing. "You're not a cop, or a teacher or anything."

I didn't like being told I wasn't anything. "I'm a private investigator."

The tiny girl halted. "You are not."

I stared at her without answering.

"Well, so what?" She took another couple steps to return to class.

"Recognize this, Amy?" I pulled out her senior picture.

Her eyes focused on the rectangle framed by my fingertips. "Where'd you get that?"

I turned it over. "*We'll see,*" I read. "To what does that refer, Amy?"

Her arm tensed, but I stuffed the photograph in my pocket before she could lunge for it.

"You stole that," she said.

I amped up my cockatrice stare. The legendary creature was hatched from a cock's egg by a serpent. It had a cock's head, an animal's body, and a snake's tail. Its breath or glance could strike you dead.

Amy did stay still and turn deathly pale.

"*We'll see* about what, Amy?"

She strode toward her classroom. "Construe whatever you want."

Construe. No wonder she was Berkeley bound.

"That doesn't have any big hidden meaning," she spit, "and you can't do anything."

"I could talk to your mom about my suspicions."

She pivoted and snorted. "Go ahead. Be prepared to get your butt chewed. My mother thinks I'm perfect."

CHAPTER 28

Watsonville's Main Street ran between the city hall and the new post office, past the notorious bars of lower Main, over the bridge, down into a fertile valley, and became the main drag through Pajaro, population 3332. The Spanish word *pajaro* meant bird, and the river, valley and town got their names because back in the 1700s the natives had presented the Spanish explorers with a bird stuffed with straw.

It made sense that Pajaro's kids walked over the bridge and the few blocks to Watsonville High School, even though the river was also a county line.

Watsonville folk ventured over to this poorer neighbor when they needed a new transmission or auto-body work. Or, on their way to the golf course, they drove by the *panaderia* where a teenage boy and his little sister had been the victims of a gangland execution, the young gunmen following the bloody, crawling boy into the bakery to make sure the job was complete. An unsolved double homicide, although plenty of people knew who'd pulled the trigger.

I drove around the town in a panic, unable to focus on the address, not because someone had shot at me, or because the neighborhood made me nervous, but because this was my last day. Noon already. I didn't have to get back to school at any particular time, but what would I do if I concluded this day with no solution to the crime? Would I call in sick and come back on Friday? Eldon would fire me. Or, Alvina Jameson would reach the end of her rope and call Officer Azevedo to bodily remove me from the campus. My husband would divorce me.

I explored to the right of the main street, slowly driving my rust bucket car through a pleasant neighborhood of small houses, fenced yards, lilies and camellias in bloom, leaves glistening from the morning's rain. I didn't find the address. I drove out on Salinas Road, past the John Deere store, Smucker's, the train yard. I finally turned into a propane company parking lot to turn around. On the other side of the town, I found low-lying brown apartments, all the same, with roosters pecking in the mud yards, the complex as poor as the often-disputed migrant camps, the underbelly of the area's billion-dollar agriculture industry.

Still I didn't find the address. I returned to the other side of town and finally located the duplex. My mom's voice chided me, "Haste makes waste." I managed to draw some deep breaths as I parked my car and forced myself not to dash up the stairs.

Lee Starling answered the door of her second-floor flat with the skeptical expression people reserve for unexpected doorbell rings. She was a surprise. Because she was white and lived in Pajaro. Because she was home. Because she was as normal and ordinary as could be. Her oval face frowned slightly. Curly, shoulder-length brown hair had a pushed-about, disheveled appearance although it had probably been brushed that morning. In spite of her daughter's death, she apparently wasn't expecting visitors. She looked about my age, which meant she'd been a very young mother. If it weren't for the peer connection, I think she would have slammed the door in my face. As it was, her hazel eyes told me that I had about fifteen seconds to convince her not to shut the door.

"I came about Jennifer."

Behind Lee Starling a female's voice asked something in rapid-fire Spanish. Lee answered in Spanish that sounded fluent and unaccented. A boy of about ten peeked over Lee's arm that held the door, barring entrance. The woman bit her lower lip, which was already red and marked from her teeth. "Are you from the school?"

"Yes." That wasn't really a lie, I rationalized. "I've been looking into Jennifer's death, but unofficially. My name's Carol Sabala."

The woman opened the door farther. Her bright purple sweatshirt advertised *Teatro Campesino* in San Juan Capistrano. "Go on, Benito. Don't stand there staring. It's not polite."

The boy had the wide-eyed, vacuous look of someone in shock.

In Spanish the boy told her to ask me for identification. The other woman, older than Lee and dressed all in black, gazed politely off to my side, but was no less busy checking me out.

"Benito, how many times have I told you that we don't speak Spanish in front of English speakers? It's rude and exclusive."

I spoke and understood Spanish in a limping way, but I usually found it to my advantage not to reveal this too soon.

"You're speaking English in front of grandma," the boy protested.

Lee sighed and glared. The boy pulled a belligerent face, but slunk down the hall where he'd probably listen to every word.

"My youngest," Lee explained, as she ushered me into a tidy living room. Blue jeans hugged her generous but firm bottom. As she led me across brown shag to a futon couch, the grandma slowly turned, her stare trailing us like a shadow. The older woman was about fifty, but in her black silence seemed a hundred.

From the couch I had a pleasant view over the town and fields to the mountains in the east. A doily-covered television in the corner had been converted into an altar. Vanilla scent swirled from a votive candle, and a large senior photograph of Jennifer smiled through a curl of smoke. Her beauty—creamy skin, intelligent eyes, sincere smile, and shiny dark hair—struck me again. A standing crucifix guarded her—Christ's face contorted in pain, lavish blood flowed from his hands and feet, blood tears trickled, exaggerated thorns in his crown pricked a circle of blood.

Lee followed my gaze. "I don't know why I'm attracted to such a garish culture. I'm an atheist myself," she said.

"*Siéntese, por favor,*" she commanded the grandma. The grandma eyed me skeptically, but then sat as commanded. Lee explained who I was and introduced the woman to me as *Señora* Huante.

The squat woman nodded respectfully, then rose. She walked proudly to the kitchen, and stirred up delicious aromas of pepper and cumin. My mouth watered. I hadn't eaten since this morning, and then, upset about Lola and the shooting, I'd managed only a half bowl of oatmeal that had tasted like glue.

"Jennifer's step-grandmother. Or, as Jenn would say, mother of asshole number three." She smiled tightly at the photo. Tears welled. "Rosa, *Señora* Huante, is the reason for this." She indicated the altar.

Lee Starling was about five-foot-four, but every inch of her, every movement, seemed to ask, "Isn't life ironic?"

"The reason we'll have a good, traditional Catholic funeral," Lee continued, "although Jenn was about as religious as I am." A net of gloom cast over the woman. "I thought Jenn going off to college was going to be hard." She chewed the swollen lip, gave an ironic bark, pressed a fist tightly to her mouth. "God, I miss her. I can't believe this."

The woman was raw, a meltdown barely contained. "Jenn used to say I wasn't satisfied with the assholes here, so I'd go down to Mexico to shop." Her mouth twitched. An attempt at a smile. "I tried to explain to her that American culture, if there is such a thing, seemed so bland to me. Baseball, hot-dogs, apple pie and Chevrolet." She swept an upturned palm as though to conjure amber waves of grain. "What are they next to *marimba, chile,* and *milagros*? *Personal cultural anthropology,* Jenn called it." Another twitch. "How she got so smart, I don't know. Her looks are from her dad. An asshole for sure, but a gorgeous one."

"Where is he now?"

She shrugged. "I don't know. Mexico, I suppose. I haven't been in touch with him for fifteen years."

"I imagine the police have been to see you."

"Oh yes." She drew herself up, crossed purple arms over her chest. "Homicide. Can you believe that? Someone killing that girl?" Her arms uncrossed and gestured dramatically at the photograph. "When I'm not thinking about Jenn, I'm thinking about what I'd like to do to the guy. Maybe something like that," she tipped her head toward the cross.

"I'd like to help you catch the killer."

"Who are you? A counselor?"

"Sort of a private investigator." I gave her a brief, honest account of how I'd come to the school and gotten entangled in Jennifer's death.

"You're a baker?"

"Well, yes, technically."

The grieved eyes inspected me all over. "And you're not even getting paid to do this?"

"Three paid days off work."

"I don't get it."

"Think of it as my *personal cultural anthropology*."

She thought about this. "The bottom line is that I'd do anything to get the guy. I loved that girl so much. My baby." She bit her lip and pressed her fist against her mouth, but couldn't punch the tears back into her head.

CHAPTER 29

I waited for Lee Starling to finish crying. The phone rang. Rosa Huante answered it, shouting, "¡*Bueno*!" like someone hard of hearing. Lee swiped her eyes and cheeks with the cuff of her purple sweatshirt. "Rosa's right off the rancho. Doesn't believe phones really work."

In the kitchen the grandmother screamed information about the time and place of the funeral.

"Do you have any suspects, Ms. Starling?"

She smiled wanly. "Oh, please, call me Lee. The cops asked that question. Ruben, that's my middle child, hangs around with gang members. I couldn't help but think of what happened at *El Nopal*. That's the bakery."

The grandmother slammed down the phone with the same ferocity she'd used to answer it. A knife chunked against wood and the smells of onion and cilantro drifted from the kitchen.

"Not that Ruben was in any way involved in those murders," Lee continued.

My mouth salivated at the delicious aroma from the kitchen. My stomach growled.

"Those killings just made me wonder if one of his rival gang members might not have gone after Jennifer. I told the cops that, which is why Ruben isn't here, but God knows where. But the more I thought about that theory, the dumber it got. That little girl in the *El Nopal* Bakery wouldn't have been shot if she hadn't been with her brother. It's not gangbanger style to seek out an uninvolved family member. And, pushing a person off a catwalk definitely isn't their style. And Mexicans are into style. Zoot Suit. Remember that? I think that movie was my downfall."

A lid clanked in the kitchen and steamy tomato and chili fragrances floated through the room. My stomach growled loudly and persistently.

Lee didn't notice. Grief wrapped her like the swaddling of a newborn baby. "So, take away the gang idea, and I'm clueless. Jennifer was so well-liked. So respected, even after she got pregnant."

"What about the father of the baby?"

"No, that's not it."

"How can you be so sure?"

Lee Starling's eyes debated. She stood. Stretched. A round, but compact woman. She stared out the window toward the mountains. Debated. Spun toward me. "I'll show you something. Something I didn't show the police."

She disappeared down the hall into which she'd banished Benito. Lee and her son argued in Spanish. Benito didn't like that she was talking to me. Didn't like what she'd said about Ruben. She didn't like the way Benito was talking to her, his mother. He should show a little more respect. If he didn't watch it, he'd turn out just like his hoodlum brother. Half-brother, Benito reminded her, and what did she expect with her lifestyle? The exchange was mean and ugly, but I admired that Lee didn't succumb for company's sake. In the end she might lose control of Benito as she apparently had with Ruben, but not without a fight.

She emerged, bristling, from the hallway, but made no apologies. "You'd think a person would learn," she muttered, "but his dad was the worst of the three." She held a dark blue, plastic-covered bankbook. She sat by me on the flowered futon and flipped up the cover. "I know two things. Jennifer's pregnancy was planned. And, she was having the baby for money." Lee pointed to the first entry. The account had been opened in November with a deposit of one thousand dollars. "That's when Jenn knew for sure she was pregnant."

Lee leaned toward me, finger running down the dates, money deposited every month. "Jennifer had a summer job, but she was using that money for this year, her senior pictures and stuff. She never even put it in the bank. I kept harping on her. Why was she applying to all these fancy colleges? Where was the money going to come from? Even if she got a full ride, which she did. That's the one time being half-Mexican helped her. I kept telling her that she'd need money for books, for food, for just plain living." Lee yelped, as though the irony had pinched her. She bit her inflamed lip to regain control. "Leave it to Jennifer. She always was resourceful. She went out and found a way to make money. Something legal that would help someone. The father wouldn't have killed her. He must have been the one paying through the nose for her to have this baby."

"What makes you think the dad paid her?"

"Who else?"

"Anyone who might really want a baby." I knew one couple who fit that bill, and they didn't include a daddy. They did include a person with a key to the catwalk. Someone Jennifer would trust.

"True. I guess I assumed the dad was involved because you know there's a man in there somewhere." She tried for a smile. "I imagined a man with an infertile wife. Something like that."

"You stressed legal. You can't just sell a baby. Can you?"

"Oh, no. Jennifer was working with a private adoption agency. That woman at school, Mrs. Goicovich, helped her to get in touch with them." This bit of information explained why Jennifer Padilla might have voluntarily subjected herself to the TAM program.

"The agency explained that they'd show Jenn letters from prospective parents," Lee Starling explained. "She'd get to choose the ones she wanted. So, the way I figure, all she had to do was let the folks who were paying her know which agency she was using, and wait for their letter to be presented to her."

"But these prospective parents wouldn't necessarily include the father of the baby," I insisted.

Lee pursed her lips and frowned. Not knowing what I did about Shayla and Becky, she didn't grasp what I was implying.

Lee Starling had already decided on a version of events for herself. "I'm not saying Jennifer had sex with the prospective father," she stammered. "Not with artificial insemination and stuff like that." She blushed to have to explain this to an adult.

"Why don't you think it might have happened the other way around, that Jennifer got pregnant and then considered the adoption?"

Lee Starling shook her disheveled hair. "Jennifer's been on birth control pills since she was sixteen. She is . . . was. . . ." She shook her head. "I can't get used to that, to *was*. She would have had to consciously stop taking her pills. If she got pregnant, it was deliberate. Why would she do that if she didn't already have the adoption idea worked out?"

The phone rang in the kitchen. Again the call seemed to be about the upcoming funeral. Lee listened for a while, but left the situation in the capable hands of Rosa.

"Okay," I relented, "but even if she got pregnant on purpose, that doesn't prove the biological father was going to adopt the baby."

I couldn't bring myself to divulge what I knew about Becky and Shayla. Their dream had been shattered. I didn't want the shards gathered for inspection, when it seemed ridiculous that either of them would have harmed the girl. Becky may have had the means, but she had no motive to murder Jennifer. She not only liked the girl, but Jennifer had been carrying, what was, I suspected, Shayla and Becky's dream child.

After a long thought, Lee conceded. "I suppose that's true. The man could have been the infertile one in the couple." Lee sighed deeply, and ran a hand through her hair, pushing the brown curls to a rakish angle from her head. "Or even if the father of the baby isn't involved in the adoption, he wouldn't kill Jennifer. Here she is . . . was, giving up the baby, no skin off his nose. And, she wouldn't tell a soul who the father was."

She had a good point. What would have been the father's motive? What was the motive for anyone to kill a pretty, smart, well-liked teenage girl? Jennifer had been a risk taker, but she hadn't deserved to die for it. She'd been trying to make money for college and to help people in the process. Each new detail painted an even more impressive portrait of Jennifer Padilla.

Lee's eyes teared again. "For the last year, I've expected someone to come to my door, to tell me Ruben was shot or dead. I never expected this." Tears drizzled down her face, already red and chaffed from salt.

Crying was an appropriate response to this tragedy, and I had no words of comfort for the woman. Nothing could be harder than losing a child. While she sobbed, I glanced at the bankbook.

CHAPTER 30

My little gray cells needed sustenance. At the same time, my type A anxiety nagged: *This is your last day. You have only hours to solve this mess.*

I'd get my sandwich to go, I rationalized and headed for Erik's Deli to the north, on the other side of Watsonville. All the efforts to revitalize downtown Watsonville ignored that the lifeblood had flowed north.

Images of a sandwich named R.E.O. Speedwagon— smoked ham, sliced turkey breast, layers of Monterey jack cheese—smothered the dates and figures of Jennifer Padilla's bankbook. Lee Starling had been sincere in her disbelief that the bankbook had a connection to Jennifer's murder, but I'd persuaded the woman to show it to the police. Jennifer had made two deposits every month.

I tried to visualize the amounts, but instead saw sprouts and red onion. My mouth thickened with saliva. I needed to remember to request horseradish. Its pungency would rush through my sinuses and clear my head. Maybe I'd go the seventy-five cents extra and add avocado.

As I passed City Hall, a police car pulled out behind me. I watched it in my rearview mirror. On this overcast Thursday, traffic was sparse on Main Street. At the plaza, only the cop, a white car, and I waited for the light. Kids trickled down Beach Street toward the school.

Erik's had good desserts, too. I could use something intense and calorie packed to get through the day. Maybe a double fudge brownie.

The light changed. Because I had a policeman behind me, I checked my rearview frequently. The police car, with the white car at a distance, stayed with me across the town. The policeman continued onto the freeway, while the white car turned left behind me, several car lengths back. The driver wore a straw hat and a kerchief around his lower face like a field worker. But a Honda Accord was hardly a field worker's car. Besides, there wasn't much to pick right now.

I turned left again, and yet again, into a shopping center. The white car slowly followed. My body sprang into full alert. Large sunglasses masked the driver's upper face. Big, probably a man, but I couldn't tell for sure. The red kerchief like a bandit's concealed features below the nose.

Everything fit. Light sedan. A Mazda or Honda, Chad had said.

My salivating mouth dried to paste. The Honda continued on to where the L-shaped lot bent toward the small shops facing Main Street. Straining to see, I twisted in the driver's seat, my bruised rib screaming in protest. The sedan stopped at the edge of my vision. When my steering wheel trembled, I thought first of an earthquake, a conditioned response from the big one of 1989. Then I realized my hands were shaking and not from low blood sugar. If someone was tailing me, he could be the killer. And he owned a gun. He'd shot off poor Lola's tail!

Had the Accord been behind me ever since Pajaro? If I were going to be a real P.I., I'd have to be more aware of such things, rather than slipping into speculations about possible evidence and choices of nine-grain wheat, light rye or peppered onion roll.

Cars jammed the lot. People threaded between the vehicles—busy workers on their lunch breaks and shoppers squeezing errands between rains. One couldn't call it broad daylight with the low gray clouds, but it hardly seemed like a time or a place that someone would attack me. But then I'd been lured into a false sense of security at the school, as my rib reminded me each time I rotated to look out the window.

People trickled in and out of Erik's and Orchard Supply Hardware.

Nothing to fear. My hand lifted to the gauze patch on my scalp. I'd given myself the same reassurance only yesterday.

My body would not get out of the car. As a matter of fact, my finger pushed down the door lock. I was afraid. And, I hated feeling that way. My stomach growled. My bruised rib told it to shut up. As I watched the white Honda, waiting for someone to disembark, the scent of Erik's "secret goo" permeated my closed windows.

My mind flashed to Lola, my poor baby shivering in the corner of the bed, hunkered behind the pillow against the wall. When I lifted her, her bloody tail hung from her body by a shred of skin. My stomach turned and roiled with anger.

I reviewed my options. I could sit here until someone discovered my skeletal remains. I could get out of the car, to be stalked, shot and killed. Or I could do like the heroes of movies. Take off. Create a chase scene, pedestrians jumping, and cars slamming into each other, shattering display windows, and exploding buildings.

I squealed out in reverse, popped my car into first, and indeed caused a young man coming from Orchard Supply Hardware to jump back, curse, and flip me the bird. I did not see a white car in hot pursuit as I spun on to Green Valley Road. I floored the gas pedal to make it through a stale yellow light at Main.

Safely through the intersection, I slowed. No white Honda followed. I thought of the person who'd located my house last night and had shot at me, the same person, no doubt, who had attacked me. Someone out there was not a Carol Sabala fan. Everyone involved in this case should be at school. Fifth period had started. But then, some people had that period as a prep. Viola Goicovich, for starters. And Ed Smith. And, Richard Goicovich, on administrative leave, had the whole day free.

I made a right on Freedom Boulevard, and headed back

toward the campus. My stomach roared with hunger. A white car burst from the parking lot of a store. My heart leapt into my throat. Had my tail taken a shortcut? I took in the shape of the old boat—*a Lincoln continental?* —crammed with people. My heart dropped back into my chest, but the adrenaline shot remained. I swerved into Burger King, a sharp, sudden move. I gunned my Ghia around the corner to the take-out window. This time my heart hit the top of my skull.

Before me was a white sedan. A Taurus. A mass of clambering kids who should have been in school whirled to check out the maniacal driver behind them. One girl in the back seat, barely visible amid the heads and tossing hair, toodled her fingers at me. I squinted at their rear window, steamed with hot breath and excitement. The girl squirmed over the others, flipped out the door, and hurried toward me as though I were her best friend. Hair streamed from her tiny body.

"Hi, Ms. Sabala!" She tried to pull open my door, but it was locked. Her doll face crinkled at me through the window. "Why's your door locked?"

I rolled down the window. "Belinda, what are you doing here?"

She giggled. "Don't worry. The cheerleaders have permission. We're thinking up a special cheer for Jennifer, for the rally tomorrow."

The idea was tackier than my mother's crocheted throws. The girls might have permission to miss fifth period, but I doubted they had permission to be at Burger King. Not that I cared. I was so hungry and relieved not to have been chased to the ground.

"You drive like my brother," Belinda announced.

"Why don't you hop in for a minute?"

The girl beamed, delighted, and threw a smug look at the teeming mass of girls in the white Taurus. She bopped to the other side of my car as I reached across to unlock the door. She dropped into the cracked seat, hitching up her ponytail to avoid sitting on her hair.

"This is such a unique car."

The Taurus inched forward and stalled, causing a frenzied tumble of bodies and unintelligible shrieking.

Belinda laughed. "That's Amy driving."

That's right, I remembered. Amy was a cheerleader, too.

"How can they be so smart and be such bad drivers?" Belinda laughed.

Amy successfully drove forward. As I pulled up to the speaker, I realized with near nauseous faintness that it might take ten minutes to get my food given the packed car in front of me. I restrained myself and ordered only a Whopper with large fries, apple pie and coffee.

Belinda made a big deal of waving to her friends. She'd shown them that she could be invited into an adult's car. I must be "cool" in some way, spotlighted because of yesterday's attack. Maybe the girls harbored romantic notions, like I did, about the thrill and glamour of investigating. However, now that Belinda and I had reached a lull in the conversation, she tensed slightly, with her diminutive fingers on the door handle, as though she were in a prison and considering escape. Giggles from the white Taurus penetrated my window. How could girls move so much in such a confined space? Amy, though, kept her face steadfastly forward.

"What kind of car does Mrs. Goicovich drive?" I asked Belinda.

The girl didn't seem puzzled by the question, maybe since we'd been vaguely on the topic of cars. She may have been relieved that I'd taken charge of making conversation.

"She has a Mazda. A red RX7," she added with relish.

"How about Mr. Goicovich?"

The girl plucked at her long hair, aware now that she was being questioned. "A mini-van," she said reluctantly, her other fingers tightened on the pitted chrome of the door handle. "I don't know what kind."

"What about Mr. Smith?"

"Dunno." She glanced toward her peers and licked her lips. "I better go. I really enjoyed your presentations."

She popped from my car, ran to the Taurus, and clambered across the bodies in the back seat, causing a new wave of whoops and hollers.

While the car full of girls waited for their bags of food, I considered Jennifer Padilla's bankbook. Sometimes Jennifer made one deposit on the first and one on the third, or one on the second and one on the sixth. Each deposit was close to five hundred dollars. Why two trips to the bank? If Shayla and Becky were making installment payments for the baby, wouldn't the deposits be farther apart? What advantage was there in giving Jennifer half the money one day, and the other half only a few days later?

CHAPTER 31

Checking my rearview every few seconds, I followed the white Taurus back to the students' parking lot out by the athletic fields. Searching for a space, Amy drove around the asphalt filled with an impressive array of cherried Volkswagens, lowered Impalas, small trucks with tinted windows, fairly new Escorts, even a couple of BMWs. Life seemed so unfair, that some teenagers could zoom around carefree in cars like these, while a kid like Jennifer Padilla devised a desperate plan to finance her college education.

The Taurus exited the lot back onto Blackburn Street, and found a slot at the remotest corner of the campus, along the field. I followed, made a U-turn and parked on the street.

The girls squirted from the Taurus like pressurized cheese. They bounced toward the campus, their heads in constant motion to see who might be watching them, their Burger King bags rolled at the top in a prissy manner, considering mine had been ripped open on my lap, the burger devoured as I drove. I exited my car, carrying my fries and apple pie in my left hand, and stopping every now and then to take a sip of the coffee in my right. Did I really want to be a private investigator? The job had to be full of Maalox moments.

Amy silently led the pack. The girls were not in cheerleading uniforms, but all in various sweat suits. Most of them carried black and gold pom-poms as well as their bags from Burger King. The group buzzed in front of me like a swarm of bumblebees. Their hair and bodies floated out, then back to center, bumping, jostling.

A big, blonde girl swung around and asked, "Are you following us?"

"Of course."

They tittered, not believing. Their hair, pulled off their faces with ribbons and scrunchies, blew behind them. Clouds scudded across the sky toward the mountains in the east. With luck, this breeze would blow the rain away.

I wanted to talk to Amy, but she was studiously ignoring me, and there were other things to check. I veered to the left, and passed the field house to the permanent portable for Teenaged Mothers. Beside it was the classroom for School Aged Parenting and Infant Development, and the playground for tikes where I'd met Jennifer. The whole dark brown affair appeared deserted. A cradle swing twisted and creaked in the rising breeze. This place, the only place where I'd seen Jennifer alive, felt as though all the life had been sucked out of it. It haunted in a way the altar in her home, even her dead body on the stage, had not. Here I felt the absence of her spirit, the poised girl across the picnic table, gone. The quick eyes, shut. The iron will, defeated.

I took the wheelchair ramp rather than the steps. The pliable wood sprang with each step as though I were walking on a trampoline.

Viola Goicovich jerked open the door and stood on the small landing. A brightly flowered skirt billowed to the front. "What do you want this time?"

I took a sip of coffee.

The chocolate eyes landed covetously on my fries and apple pie. If all I had for lunch were a pippin, I'd be crabby, too, I decided. "I just wanted to see if you were here."

"Well here I am." She crossed bare arms over a pale blue shell.

Since both of my hands were full, I grabbed a French fry with my teeth and slurped it like spaghetti.

I quickly chewed and swallowed. "What kind of car does Ed Smith drive?"

"What kind of question is that?" Even with the breeze whipping blonde curls across her face, Viola appeared too composed to have been pursuing me all lunch hour.

"Just curious," I said.

"Yeah, right." The woman glowered down at me. "How would I know what kind of car Ed drives?"

I didn't expect Viola Goicovich to embrace me, but this response seemed unnecessarily defensive.

"Isn't Ed good friends with your husband?"

"That doesn't mean I know what kind of car he drives." Viola's skirt whirled with colors like a peacock's tail. The hypnotic display disappeared, and the door slammed.

Touchy. I fished another fry with my teeth. I didn't believe that she had no idea about the make of a friend's car. She clearly just didn't want to tell me. Why? I took a big slurp of coffee before heading down the ramp. It sprang and sang like a played saw.

Viola felt some need to protect Ed. Did she know something that implicated him? Was she evasive because the man was her husband's friend? Could it be that whatever she'd felt for Ed in high school had never completely dissolved? Or, I supposed the woman could simply not like me. My mom would consider that eminently possible.

I crossed the Maple Street extension to the other side of the school's outer reaches. Behind the auto shop and art buildings was the faculty parking lot. I wound through the cars. There was a white Accord, but it was encrusted in dry mud. The car behind me hadn't been noticeably dirty. The lot was full. If my pursuer had returned to the campus, he'd probably been forced to park on the street as we had. He might have chosen that option to avoid detection even if the lot weren't full.

Across Lincoln Street, the cheerleaders sat on the steps in front of one of the entrances into the gym. Their Burger King feasts lay on papers in their laps and on the concrete. Lincoln Street was deserted between the orange and white sawhorses at each end of the block, so I strolled in my best cool, nonchalant way toward the group. "I see you're getting a lot of practice," I said.

The big blond girl and Belinda smiled at me. Two Hispanic girls inspected me. Amy and the other two ignored me. Apparently they were all impervious to the cold dampness of the concrete.

"We have to have nourishment to do our routines," the big girl explained.

"I can't flip on an empty stomach," said Belinda.

I couldn't imagine flipping on anything else, but then, I was no longer a teenager.

"Amy, I need to talk to you," I said.

"Been there. Done that," she muttered, barely turning her head.

The two girls with Amy took their cues from her and two sets of dark eyes glared at me. One of them whispered something to Amy that contained the word bitch.

I drained my coffee, deposited the cup in a dented and graffitied trashcan, and with my now free right hand extracted Amy's senior picture. "I guess, then, that I'll just have to continue our discussion in front of your friends."

Her head shot up, the delicate face scowling. "This is harassment." She stood, though.

Frowning, her two cohorts peered up at her, and I realized they were twins, with flawless brown faces, honey-brown hair tied back with black and gold ribbons, ample breasts tugging black sweatshirts away from the pants. They awaited Amy's direction.

"I'll be right back," she said. "Practice the death plunge with Belinda."

Death plunge. The words gave me goose bumps, but apparently didn't resonate for the girls.

Amy led the way around the corner, toward the pool, her step bouncy in athletic shoes. A gold and black pom-pom braceleted her right wrist and rustled as she walked. She stopped at the far corner of the gym, looked toward the pool, back toward Lincoln Street, and across the quad. "What do you want this time?" she snarled.

"The truth."

Amy was a fierce little creature, but she came up only to my shoulder, and even though she was in fine physical form, I could probably break her in half.

"I haven't told you any lies."

"A smart girl like you knows about lies of omission."

"I don't feel like I have to tell people stuff that isn't any of their business."

"Even when your friend gets killed?"

"The two things are not connected."

"How can you be so sure?"

She hesitated, and an amazing thing happened. A shaft of sun broke through the clouds and shone on Amy, as though she were in a spotlight, or as though God had cast an eyebeam on her directly from heaven. With her back covered by the gym, the girl checked in every direction again. She'd chosen this spot with the street smarts of a modern teenager, an intelligence not measured by test scores. "I'm gonna tell you this, and then I want you to leave me alone," she hissed.

I couldn't promise her that, so I said nothing. Detectives-in-training can lie by omission, too.

"You seem to have figured it out, anyway," she muttered. "Goicovich suggested that we could 'work something out' on my grade."

"And you were considering it?"

She looked at her shoes, and then her head tipped up in defiance. "My whole future was on the line." She sighed deeply. "Anyway, it's not like I'm a virgin or anything. Or like he's gross or anything."

"Jennifer knew, didn't she?"

"Yeah."

"And you two got in a fight about it?"

"Yeah."

Amy stiffened, as though realizing the implication, the danger. "Oh, no, you don't think . . . can't think." Her hand flew to her black hair. The pom-pom burst alive, the gold glittering in the sun, its rattle startling both of us. "The police asked me about my hair, of course, but that was so obvious. I'd been brushing my hair in the green room just that day. You know. You saw me." The black and gold pom-pom dropped back to the side of her sweatpants.

"Relax, Amy. I don't think that you killed your friend. Because she was your friend, a good friend, and you know it." My fingers cramped around the remaining fries and apple pie. The food no longer radiated any warmth.

Amy's face crumpled like a dried petal, no more bright hostility, just pale, defeated tissue. She didn't cry. Her denial about Jennifer's death had been so deep that she hadn't passed yet through realization and shock, which fell on her now like the sunbeam.

"She didn't want me to do it," Amy whispered. "We got in a big fight about it. She wanted me to join with her in the sexual harassment charge. But I told her two could play at his little game."

I put my free hand on the girl's shoulder. "Look, Amy, I don't plan to talk to your mom about this. I think Jennifer was killed by someone who was trying to pay her off, but then changed his mind. Or, maybe Jennifer was blackmailing him."

"Who?"

"The baby's father."

"The big mystery."

CHAPTER 32

The sun had popped out bright enough to warm my face. "So, Goicovich suggested the two of you meet on the catwalk?"

"No," Amy paused. "I suggested it. And we weren't going to meet on the catwalk," she said with a trace of scorn at the idea of "doing it" on the floor of the catwalk. "There's a projection room up there. It has a couch in it and everything."

"So, what I need to know, Amy, is how you got up there."

"Security is not as tight as Ms. Rivas would like everyone to believe. She's way too stressed to pay attention to everything."

"Are you saying that she didn't lock the door and is trying to cover her butt?"

The girl thought about my suggestion, a moment too long. "You sure jump to conclusions," she charged.

"Both my husband and mom would concur."

She smiled weakly at that. "Well, that's not it."

"What is it?" I demanded, forgetting any interviewing technique I'd ever known.

Her eyes inspected something off to the side of my face. "I don't think this is relevant."

"Why not?" Impatience edged my voice. "At the very least, the unlocked door allowed Jennifer to be at the place where she met her death."

The girl gulped, the up and down visible on her slender golden neck. "Well," she said hesitantly, "you think the murderer was the father of Jenn's baby. So it wasn't Goicovich. I happen to know he had a vasectomy."

"Amy!" I barked, out of patience.

Her hand flew up again, to shield herself from the verbal attack, and the pom-pom leaped with it. I jumped back as though it were a Doberman going for my throat. I wished she'd take the damn thing off.

But Amy wasn't thinking about me. Her eyes darted as though in a REM dream. She was thinking fast about whether to lie, or to plunge forward on this path of confession.

"I stuck a wad of masking tape in the hole thingy."

All this subterfuge. Had my generation been like this in high school? No wonder she'd turned such doleful eyes on me the day of Jennifer's death. She might have provided Jennifer, the murderer, or both, access to the scene of the crime.

"Hole thingy?" I asked. Even teenagers bound for Cal were still teenagers.

We heard the slightly whiny voice calling Amy's name before the twin appeared around the corner of the gym.

"Whatdaya want?" Amy growled.

The worshipful, voluptuous girl kept a distance.

"We can't do the death plunge without you."

"Oh don't be a wuss, Danielle," Amy snapped. "Of course you can." Her voice was impatient, but it also imparted one hundred percent confidence in her squad.

The girl turned reluctantly. Dismissed.

I saw Amy's leadership and courage. Go practice the death plunge without me. You can do it. Just like that. While I imagined Belinda splatted on the beautiful wood floor of the gym, Amy had no fear. Whether I approved or disapproved of her actions, this was a gutsy girl, ready to go toe-to-toe with a teacher, to exploit his vice.

"So, hole thingy?" I prodded. I made my voice as gentle as possible, but sounded like my mom. My mom delivered her clichéd words of wisdom like Jonathan Edwards, full of judgment. I wondered if high school kids still read *Sinners in the Hands of an Angry God*. I'd hated it, but I'd never forgotten it.

"You know, the hole the key turns the latch into," she mumbled. Now that the truth was out, she looked at me, an impressive tear welling at the corner of her eye. "Goicovich could have gotten a key. The president of the Arts Council was a Goicovich. His sister, I think. But part of his whole trip was making me jump through hoops."

The tear swelled to cartoon proportions. The girl should be an actress, I thought, and then I remembered that she was. She flicked away the tear with her pom-pommed hand, startling me a third time with its bright rustle.

"Let me tell you something," Amy's voice sounded like a hammer on nails and her eyes flipped up at me. Dewy as they were, these were not the eyes of a damsel in distress. They were fierce. I remembered what Arturo had said about her. That she dropped bombs. I could, at that moment, imagine her as a kamikaze. I braced myself.

"Goicovich is a slime," she said bitterly, "but he's a subtle one. No one's ever going to get him." Big tears swelled in her eyes. There was nothing phony about them. They leaked down her lovely face. "I should have listened to Jenn. I am so sorry I didn't support her. I. . . ."

She was crumbling, and I wanted to embrace her, but we both came from traditions of reserve and propriety. She pulled her tiny body straight and swiped at the tears.

"He's just laughing at me, all cocky and secure. If I said anything now about the sexual harassment, no one would believe me. Everyone would just think I was trying to get him because of the cheating thing."

I suddenly saw the full reason for Amy's anger. The reason she'd been crying on the catwalk. "He didn't show up, did he, Amy?"

She shook her head hard, swaying the black silk of her hair. "No, he didn't. That was his whole idea from the beginning." She glared at me as though I could be Goicovich. "It's just like they taught us in health class about rapists. It's not about sex.

It's about power. I thought he lusted for my body," she castigated herself. "I flattered myself that he was going to great lengths to get it. But you know what?"

I murmured sympathetically.

"It was just the opposite. He didn't want my body. He wanted to humiliate me."

The barrier between us fell away. The girl cried in earnest, and there was nothing to do except enfold her tiny body in my arms.

CHAPTER 33

The shrilling bell, slamming doors, and stomping feet drove us apart. We were both embarrassed, but bonded. Allies now.

"Did you remove the masking tape, Amy?"

She shook her head, then leaned against the gym's stucco, bent over, and unlaced her high-top cross trainer. She didn't seem to want her peers to think we were together. At a time like this, the teenager sensibility was maddening. She propped herself on one foot, back against the stucco, took off the other shoe, and shook it out.

The extravagance of her silence made me look around. Arms crossed over his massive chest, Ed Smith stood by the pool's fence, ostensibly talking to a student, but glowering at us over the student's head of black curls. The body movements of the girl talking to him seemed supple, persistent, and flirtatious. Ed wore black sweat shorts, one of the advantages, I thought, of being a P.E. teacher. Amy put the shoe back on, taking exaggerated care with the gold and black laces as kids streamed past us, some greeting her.

From the corner of my eyes I became aware of a black and gold swarm headed our way. Amy was aware of them, too.

"If you didn't remove the tape, I wonder why the police didn't find it? No one's mentioned it." With the blabbermouth Officer Azevedo around campus and the cops interviewing kids, information and misinformation spread across the campus like the plague. I thought about how Viola knew there was skin under Jennifer's nails, how Chendo repeated the cause of death, how everyone seemed to know Amy's hair had been on the body. But, no one had mentioned a blob of masking tape.

Amy was not answering, and I snapped out of my thoughts to focus on her. Her head tilted, first toward Ed Smith, whose eyes were fixed on us so that I could feel their gray stoniness forty feet away. Amy's gaze flicked in warning toward the approaching group of girls. Then her eyes beamed right at me. The message was clear. I was being totally uncool about something. I had no idea what.

"Are you thinking about going up there?" she asked in a stage whisper.

I nodded. "I have to know now if the tape is still there." If it were, the police had not done their job. If it weren't, that probably meant they had found it and considered it significant evidence, information they intentionally withheld, waiting for someone to incriminate him or herself. Either way, Amy was in trouble.

"Be careful," she warned.

"Wanna come?"

She considered it as her cheerleading buddies collected to the side of us.

"I better go to English." She spoke now in a voice slightly louder than normal, although the crowd was thinning as students made their way to sixth period. "I can't afford to do any worse in there."

"Go in the weight room and start lifting," Ed Smith growled at a group of three boys sauntering in his direction. One of them wore a sweatshirt that announced he was a wrestler. "Where's Arturo?" Ed Smith asked angrily.

Amy hesitated, listening to this exchange.

The wrestlers shrugged in unison. "English class, I guess," one of them muttered. One didn't tattle, not even to a coach.

"English," Coach Smith spat. "They have a sub. He doesn't need to go to that."

Boy, I thought, a person could get away with a lot if he were a former campus star with a present star team. Before Amy escaped, I tried Ed's logic on her. "I hate to admit that jerk might be right," I tipped my head toward Smith, "but I peeked in one of Goicovich's classes with a sub. It didn't look to me like you or Arturo would miss much unless you're in the hacky-sack tournament."

Her eyes cut me an insistent get-a-life, get-a-clue stare. I looked all around me but whatever the message was, my over-thirty antennae failed to receive it.

"We have a test on Hamlet today," Amy said loudly. "Act II."

"We do?" one of the twin cheerleaders squeaked from the sidelines. If this weren't Amy, their leader, they clearly would not have continued to wait.

Amy glared at her cohort.

The girl heaved a big sigh, pom-poms on her hips. "Come on, Amy," she whined. "We're gonna be late."

"Go without me, Dawn," Amy said.

I didn't know how she could tell this twin from the other one, Danielle, except this one seemed to have a little more backbone. She didn't leave at Amy's command. "Are you on the rag, or what?" she said snottily. "We needed your help at practice, you know."

"Don't get caught," Amy mouthed to me before turning to join her clique. "If you run into Arturo, be sure to remind him about the test," she added, as the band of long-haired beauties bebopped past and headed across the quad.

Someone had put fresh soil in the empty squares awaiting trees. They reminded me of graves.

The campus cleared. As I walked across the new concrete, already marked with black gum droppings, I considered Amy and Goicovich. He could have gotten a key to the catwalk, but hadn't. According to Amy, he was too clever, too subtle, to leave a trail like that, so he wouldn't have borrowed a key to meet and to kill Jennifer.

Instead, just as he had done with Amy, he would have insisted Jennifer open the doors, both to the green room and to the catwalk, easy enough with her cleverness and position as House Manager for the play. According to Amy, security had not been as tight as Becky Rivas would like to have people believe. Goicovich would have known that Amy had the doors opened that day, but he couldn't be certain she'd leave them unlocked after he stood her up. As a matter of fact, he'd figure they weren't unlocked. Which brought me back to the fact that he wasn't the type to borrow a key.

Goicovich treasured the male version of power—dominance. Not my idea of power at all. Real power came from confidence in oneself, and those confident in themselves didn't need to oppress others. Richard Goicovich would hate for someone else to have the upper hand. He might kill a blackmailer. But, why would Jennifer blackmail him? He wasn't the baby's father, couldn't have been. Unless he spread a story of his vasectomy for his own purposes. That would explain why Viola had never mentioned it. The final bell shrilled.

"Carol!" a voice called.

I looked up.

Alvina Jameson, who had been striding like an ostrich from the lounge toward her classroom, turned and loped toward me. "Carol, what did you do?"

What did I do? Something drastic, given the urgency of Alvina's voice and the fact she was now galloping toward me in spite of her waiting class.

"Javier came at lunch and cleaned those windows!" In spite of her kindness, Alvina seemed oblivious that she was shouting this announcement to the entire campus. "He said that you'd explain." She wanted an explanation and right now.

I could think of nothing but one of my mother's clichés. "Miracles never cease."

Alvina rounded the library and halted. "Come talk to me after school," she said eagerly, doing an abrupt about-face, and hurrying toward her room. Whatever motivational secret I possessed, she lusted for it.

Extortion worked wonders.

A student straggler sauntered across the quad from the gym area, checked his watch, raised his head toward the lollipop sun, sighed wistfully, then headed toward a classroom door. A couple of girls emerged from the front of the main building, glanced around, saw me, conferred, decided I was insignificant, and headed toward the street to cut class. Their action reminded me of volleyball when I jumped to block, but a player on the opposing team called to his hitter, "No one." That always pushed a button.

A stocky man wearing shorts appeared in the middle of the quad. The rest of his attire included an athletic jacket advertising the Junior All Stars and an A's baseball cap. He carried a two-way radio. With a smile, I pointed toward the street. "Two cutters, heading toward Main." That was almost as satisfying as getting a touch on the volleyball after the opponent referred to me as no one. The campus supervisor grinned and hiked toward Beach Street to see what he could see, a couple of cutters apparently not enough to get his mojo working. I was glad not to have him see me try the door to the green room. It was locked, but I could hear hammering inside. I pounded on the door. Arturo Arteaga opened it.

The room smelled of fresh-cut wood and sawdust powdered the floor. Arturo settled on the floor, legs splayed, and like a child with a truck, played with what he'd been building.

"Pretty cool, huh?" he asked, again like the pleased child, but with a deep, booming voice that matched his bullish neck and the muscles of a heavyweight wrestler.

I tried to concentrate on what Arturo was showing me, a cart on casters, but I was thinking about how Jennifer was thrown from the catwalk. How there was so little physical evidence, as though her attacker had been someone she trusted. Someone strong. Someone who could hurtle her over that rail before she even clawed him. I thought of Amy, who knew Jennifer as well as anybody, suggesting Arturo as the father of the baby. Handsome. Age-appropriate.

"This is for a palm tree." Arturo pointed to a jungle of artificial tropical trees leaning against the far wall, the back of the stage. "These will not only hold the trees up," he said proudly, "but we'll be able to roll them on and off or wherever we want."

"Cool."

"You should see the trees already on the stage. We're hot gluing on fronds that project forward so the trees are three-dimensional."

"Aren't you supposed to be in English right now?"

He gave me a what's-it-to-you expression, but explained politely, "We have a sub."

"How did you get in here?"

His large brown eyes gave me a repeat of the look. "Ms. Rivas let me in at the end of lunch." He seemed too well mannered to be all out rude to an adult, especially a female one.

"Did Ms. Rivas give you the key?"

"No. Of course not." He studied me with a peculiar expression and stood. He lied as badly as I did. "As you know, the door's locked from the outside. All I have to do is shut it behind me."

I wanted to get rid of this guy. Now that he was standing, his muscles made me nervous.

His eyes narrowed. "So, what are you doing here?" He dusted off the butt of his baggy jeans and stepped toward me.

What if he were the father of Jennifer's baby? The murderer. The in-style sloppiness of his billowing purple shirt didn't conceal the depth of his chest, the power in his build.

"You know, Amy Hirahara just told me you're having a test on Act II of *Hamlet* today."

He frowned. "What?"

"Yeah, she was so concerned about it she wouldn't even come over here with me."

He wiped his palms on his baggies. "No shit?" He glanced down at his project. "I mean . . . sorry. It just slipped out. Really? Why didn't I know that?"

I shrugged, glad that I didn't have to lie. I was getting better at it, but I had the definite disadvantage of not being brought up with the skill.

"Amy said that?"

"She did." Arturo seemed so perplexed by this information that I wondered if Amy had lied to me. But why would she lie about a test on *Hamlet*?

The worried eighteen-year-old before me didn't make sense as the murderer. How would he get the money necessary to pay off Jennifer? Why would he bother? From the number of unmarried girls in the TAM program, and from what Viola had told me, getting a girl pregnant didn't seem to cramp any boy's lifestyle.

Arturo plucked up his Bulls jacket, revealing a stack of cut two by fours. "Drat. I was planning to get all these done." He spoke with a preoccupied voice, as though already lost in the complexities of *Hamlet*. He drifted toward the door. "Make sure this is shut when you leave."

CHAPTER 34

The door clicked. I was alone. I took a moment to clear my head. This was the final hour of my final day, and I was here to check on a blob of masking tape. If it were in the. . . . What was the "hole thingy" called? Shit! I slapped my face to get my attention. If the tape were here, well, it proved only that anybody who could have gotten into the auditorium could have also gotten onto the catwalk. *Great.* But, at least, I'd be able to get a peek at the true crime scene. Maybe it would suggest something to me. I didn't have any better idea where to go next.

If the tape weren't there, I'd assume the police had it, although the murderer could have removed it, smirking all the while.

I moved around the wall to the stage proper and was stunned by the darkness of the theater. It was like staring into a well. The light from the green room revealed outlines of props near me, but I couldn't even tell what they were. Blindness heightened my other senses. My nose picked up the electrical, intoxicating, slightly sweet odor of a hot glue gun. An errant set builder must have left it plugged in.

I waited for my eyes to adjust. The door to the catwalk was somewhere on the other side of the stage. I peered into blackness, darker than a moonless night. I hadn't realized that the performing arts center had no windows. My eyes didn't adjust at all. I retreated to the green room. The stage had lights. With illogical hope, I searched for the switches in the green room where they'd be easy to see. I didn't look long.

A key clicked in the door. I slid around the wall to the stage. I didn't want to be caught in here, not even by Becky, a friend, and definitely not by the person who'd been pursuing me.

Somewhere in front of me the stage dropped into the orchestra pit. It seemed as though entertainers, like Gloria Esteban, regularly fell off stages, spraining their ankles or rupturing discs in their backs. As far as I knew, they tumbled from regular stages into surging masses of fans, not from stages that dropped another six feet into the hard bottoms of pits. The distance to the pit floor wasn't as far as Jennifer Padilla had fallen, but it wasn't a leap I wanted to make accidentally. Or on purpose.

The green room door closed. Big steps crossed purposefully toward the stage. I shrank toward the props, but the more I moved into the darkness, the less certain I was of my direction. The shadowy light from the green room provided my only orientation. I thought again of the pit and got down on my hands and knees. The wooden floor was gritty with dust. I crawled behind a prop.

The steps clomped. A man's. Another stereotype. How did I know they were a man's? I wasn't sure, but most women, even if high heels had gone the way of vinyl records, learned to walk lifting their weight out of their feet. Stereotypes contained truth. Some women probably did walk like flat-footed bears, but most of them didn't.

My escapist thoughts, meant to distract me from my trembling body, ceased as the heavy steps thumped onto the stage. If the person knew where the lights were, he didn't turn them on. I cowered behind the prop and worked up the courage to try to find its edge so I could peek around it. I put my hand on it to explore. It fell away from me. I realized that it was cardboard— an unpropped prop—at the same time my body lurched after it, skim boarding across the stage. This cheap thrill wrenched my underarm and gave me an ungentle reminder of my bruised rib.

The steps moved confidently toward the noise, part of which had been a groan of pain. I was in deep shit.

I pulled myself into a balanced crouch. Except for the rib, I was strong and fit, with a vertical jump that could put my hands over an eight-foot volleyball net and block a male attacker. Unfortunately, a volleyball block wasn't about to incapacitate anyone. And I would have to debilitate this person somehow, because this wasn't Officer Azevedo or a student come to work on the props. The dim shape that towered before me was the killer, come to kill again.

CHAPTER 35

He chuckled. This pissed me off. My body flamed with adrenaline, which burned away some of the fear. My mother considered my temper and rashness my worst qualities, but right now, they were proving useful. I didn't know who stood before me. He was dressed in dark clothing. The prop no longer separated me from the faint light, but he was backlit just enough to inform me he was big.

Doug, the custodian? He had a key. He also surely knew where the lights were, and wouldn't it be easier to kill me if he could see what he was doing? Besides, while he seemed lascivious enough to have an affair with a student, I couldn't see Jennifer having an affair with him, even if her intention had simply been to get pregnant.

The shadowy outline crouched, and moved from side to side like a cobra. The thought of Jennifer hurled to her death, then of the boot kicking my rib, and my poor Lola with her tail shot off, turned my anger to rage. I fought an urge to charge stupidly at my predator.

Think, I commanded myself. This must be somebody who didn't have to be in class. *Goicovich?*

Thinking, unfortunately, quelled my fury, and with it, my blind bravery. I resisted the temptation to move backward. The shadowy figure feinted from side to side. *Why didn't he launch at me?*

I forced myself into my center, weight forward onto the balls of my feet, as though preparing to receive a hard-spiked volleyball, the position meant for quick movement. I hoped to be faster, to dodge his assault, and not to drop into the orchestra pit. My only advantage was the dim light to his back. I could see his outline. But in my black jacket and jeans, I couldn't be easy to see. I held my breath.

The man crouched in a low stance, the body moving cobra-like, all familiar. And I knew it wasn't Goicovich as the dark form lunged toward my leg. I pivoted and he missed, but his weight hit my calf and I slammed sideways onto the wooden floor. Goicovich hadn't used a key with Amy, and he wouldn't use a key now. This guy was less subtle. *Why wasn't he in class?*

His rolling shoulders and lunge were familiar because I'd seen them back in high school. Back when my dear, athletic, gay brother had been alive, trying to hide his homosexuality by participating in every sport devised by man. This was the movement of a wrestler. In spite of the fact his take down had not worked as intended, my assailant was perfectly balanced and turned, while I lay, sprawled in pain on the floor. I flipped onto my back.

"Time to take a little accidental fall into the pit," he said.

"Not very imaginative."

"Why fool with success?" he asked in his gravelly voice.

I pedaled my legs as though frantically riding a bike, hoping at least to be a difficult, moving target.

He laughed.

My pumping legs propelled me backward a few inches and my arm bumped into something. I didn't stop to wonder what it was. Anything, anything at all, was a weapon. I reached for it as Ed Smith caught my legs and whipped me onto my stomach, knocking the wind out of me. Pain seared my rib cage. I latched onto a hard cylinder and burned my finger. I knew what the object was. I'd smelled it earlier. I yanked at the hot glue gun that someone had left plugged in as Ed Smith's two hundred pounds came down on my back. The glue gun came freely as though plugged into an extension cord. I remembered Lola. The kick to my ribs. My movement was too restricted to bring my arm around into his face as I would have liked. I settled for jabbing the hot, metal tip into his bare thigh.

"Jesus! You goddamn bitch!"

His right hand floundered, flying toward the pain and then reversing course toward my right arm, enough time to retract my arm, and to fling it upward from the elbow, the burning metal tip connecting in a sickening, satisfying way with his bent upper body.

His strong hands flew away from me, but I still had two hundred pounds of dead weight squashing me against the floor. "Jesus Christ! You fuckin' bitch. You're going to die now."

As if murder hadn't been his intention from the beginning. His upper body weight crushed into me, his arms found mine and slid along the tops of them. A meaty clamp flicked my wrist and sailed the weapon from my hand. The glue gun clattered on the stage.

Ed Smith's hot breath puffed in my ear. "You snoopy bitch. I wish that I could have used some finesse, the way I did with Jennifer. That was a flawless suplex. Sometimes called a soufflé," he panted in my ear. "I leaned backward and flipped her over that rail like a little bird."

He may have once been a great wrestler, but Ed Smith was winded. He pressed his groin into my thighs.

I tried to buck, but couldn't lift my body at all. I was pinned.

He chuckled. "Why do I always like bitches?" He spread my legs with his knee.

If I'd had a gun, if I'd had a way, I would have killed him. Think, think, think, I berated myself. If he wanted me accidentally to fall into the orchestra pit, he had to get me from where we were to the edge of the stage. I needed to stall, to plot, to take advantage of that moment. "Why did you do it?"

"With two ex-wives, alimony and child support," he said, "there's no way I could pay that little bitch five hundred bucks every month on a crappy teacher's salary."

His perception of himself as a victim was the final straw. I couldn't abide whiners, even when they had something to whine about. "You deserve the salary of a crappy teacher," I said, letting rashness win. If I were going to die, I may as well have the last word. Exit the world as stubbornly as I had entered.

Ed Smith twisted my right arm behind me. Tears sprang to my eyes. My head jerked involuntarily against the cold, gritty floor.

"I've produced wrestling champs. What have you ever produced? Besides cookies?" he sneered.

I felt sick to my core. He had a point. Even if he got caught for killing, some people would reminisce "but he was a good teacher." The wrongness infuriated me. He was not a good teacher—he was a cold-blooded murderer. I didn't care how many wrestling champs he'd coached.

"If I didn't want this to look like an accident, I'd snap this little arm." He added pressure, and I whimpered in spite of myself.

"Like that, do you?" he breathed in my ear. "Lucky for you," he paused to kiss and suck my earlobe, "I want the injuries to look consistent with a fall."

I hated the condescension of "little arm," and his erotic pleasure in domination, but maybe it was because my other ear was crushed to the floor and he was busy slurping that I heard the door and he didn't.

CHAPTER 36

The patter of feet inspired Ed Smith to raise his head and decide that he'd better kill me while he had a chance. He wrenched me up in front of him with my arms pinned behind me. Then he hesitated. He had no more idea than I did which way to go to the pit, and if he went the wrong way, he could fall in first. The darkness was so complete that I wondered if the stage curtain were shut.

"Damn," Ed Smith whispered. His voice sounded panicked.

The steps moved confidently from the green room to the side of the stage. Two figures emerged into the shadowy light.

"I caught this woman trespassing, destroying the set," Ed Smith said, his voice aggressive and confident again.

"That is a complete lie," I countered to our unknown audience.

The lights whirred and flickered and filled the stage, as miraculous to me as the first day of creation. The world before us was a mess. I'd knocked over a cardboard volcano. An orange extension cord wound across the stage, a broken glue gun at the end. Sawdust and dirt covered my clothes. I was happy to see that while Ed Smith might break my arms with one swift movement, he'd have to march me at least twenty feet before he could toss me into the orchestra pit.

"Don't move another step," Amy Hirahara hissed at Ed Smith. "I know hapkido."

I laughed, probably hysterical. But the line, delivered by this tiny Japanese girl to the mass of muscle I could feel even through my padded jacket, belonged in a B movie. Make that a C movie. Fortunately, Amy had brought Arturo Arteaga with her.

Amy glared at us.

"Don't just stand there, Arturo," Ed Smith said. "Go get Officer Azevedo."

Arturo cast a mournful face at his coach. He glanced doubtfully at Amy, but she didn't take her eyes from us. *Smart girl.* I berated myself for my initial reaction. Who was to say that Amy might not be the better rescuer of the two? Here was another of my damn stereotypes, thinking I needed a man in shining armor to save me.

Arturo's sad eyes returned to their gaze slightly over my head to his coach's face. "You killed Jennifer." The deep baritone sounded questioning. He wanted to be convinced this weren't true. He stepped away from Amy's side toward the edge of the stage, but he didn't come toward us.

"Yeah, right, Arturo," Ed Smith said sarcastically. "This drama business has given you an overactive imagination. I tell you that this woman was snooping around in here, breaking stuff. Just look at this mess."

I considered a backward kick into his shin, but the alertness in the powerful legs pressing my thighs told me he'd pound my face into the floor if I tried.

"Why don't you release Ms. Sabala?" Amy calmly suggested. "It looks like she's wrecked everything there is to wreck. There are three of us to subdue her if she tries anything."

Oh, my dear, sweet, bright, Cal-bound girl, I thought.

If the psychopath would let me go, there would be three of us to overpower him. Maybe. Arturo's eyes ping-ponged between Amy and his coach. He took another step to the side, and I wondered what the hell he was doing.

"I think she may be armed," Ed Smith said.

The ease with which he spun his story astonished me. My mother had raised me on maxims like George Washington's "honesty is always the best policy." Reality did seem hard enough without getting caught in a web of lies. Still, I wished I were a little better prepared for spiders like Ed Smith.

"I'll frisk her," Amy volunteered, but she stayed put. Amy may have been younger and less experienced than I was, but she was a brighter person. She'd been quicker to grasp that for all his glib lies, Ed Smith was desperate. Wrapped in his arms, his strong legs tensed behind mine, his breath hot on the crown of my head, I was snared like a fly.

"So, Coach," Arturo stepped farther to the side, and took a step toward us.

Ed Smith jacked my forearms another fraction of an inch up my back. I winced.

"What were you doing here?" Arturo sidestepped, and edged forward again.

Jesus, stop, before he snaps my arms, I thought.

"I came to find you," Ed Smith said. "For weight training."

While the coach had been busy spinning lies, believing that he could sway one of his boys, Arturo had put enough distance between himself and Amy so that Ed Smith could not focus on both of them. He'd also positioned himself between the edge of the stage and us.

"Sorry, Coach, I actually went to English. We had a test on *Hamlet.*" Humor warmed his deep voice. This was an inside joke that I didn't comprehend, but I felt certain there'd been no test.

All of this had been Amy's strategy. She'd suspected Ed Smith, had known he might follow me, had tried to warn me back at the gym, and as a last resort had insured that Arturo would come to English class so that she could talk to him first. Then she'd have backup and a way into the green room. Apparently Ms. Rivas had left Arturo with a key.

Arturo crouched. Ed Smith's body rotated toward him, swiveling me, his appendage. My peripheral vision glimpsed a flying body, black hair streaming behind her, leg out. The force landed effectively on the side of Ed Smith's knees. He buckled.

I struggled. I didn't pull free, but the extra jerk caused Ed to fall, me on top of him.

Arturo yanked the arms from mine and pinned them. "Get his legs!" he shouted.

Disoriented, I sat on the man's legs, but the right one popped free. It cocked and lashed out, the heel landing in my solar plexus. I fell back on to the floor. Yellow lights pricked the brownness before me, and tears sprouted.

Then I heard a groan. Another. And another. My vision cleared. Tears trickled down my cheeks. Amy Hirahara was avenging me. And Jennifer. All the anger over her friend's death moved into her foot and out through the athletic shoe into Ed Smith's groin and pelvis and legs until I started to become afraid she might kill him.

I grabbed the extension cord, and while Arturo held Ed Smith's arms, and Amy, panting, made sure he didn't try anything fancy with his legs, I hogtied his ankles.

"Can you two hold him while I find Officer Azevedo?" I asked.

"I better go," Amy said. She wiped her forehead with her sweatshirt sleeve. "You don't know your way around."

"Good thinking." Even though the bulk of her anger seemed spent, I was relieved to see her go.

While the girl trotted down the steps and exited a side door of the auditorium, Arturo's dark eyes flicked up at me. "See why I call her Hiroshima?"

I bit my lip and nodded, preoccupied with my pain and own thoughts. I vowed that I would never again listen passively as people maligned "kids nowadays."

CHAPTER 37

I sat in the dark. The plush green seat embraced me. I tried to concentrate on *South Pacific*, but a jumble of thoughts and feelings tugged my attention away.

Zack, who'd become the house manager, had announced the dedication of the show to Jennifer. There was no cause to go into sordid details. Everybody in the community knew them. The scandal had been front-page news on both Watsonville's and Santa Cruz's local papers. This was part of the reason the seat beside me was empty.

Memories of my last time in the theater asserted themselves, an illusion overlaid on the illusion of the play. Amy pounding about the stage and chortling as Bloody Mary became a double exposure with Amy flying through the air, one leg of her black sweat suit extended like a javelin, the other bent behind her. My body remembered Ed Smith's foot in my gut, and I jerked. Maybe I was glad, after all, that I was seated between the aisle and an empty seat. Anyone too near might have thought I had Tourette's Syndrome.

My gaze floated, trying to see above the curtain line to the mysterious catwalk. The police had found Amy's wad of masking tape. They'd considered it "significant." But like much of life, the evidence misled. Ed Smith had used his ex-wife Charlene's master key, never noticing that the door to the cat-walk wasn't locked. Ironically, if he'd known about the unlocked door and the number of suspects that allowed, he wouldn't have felt so threatened by my investigation.

Arturo, Amy and I had become folk heroes of a sort. When I'd entered the gracious, tiled lobby, I'd felt people watching and pointing at me. In spite of a milling crowd, the lobby had felt oddly empty, the way a place can when you are held at a distance from others. The color scheme was the warm peach and forest green of the exterior, but the ceiling was high, and there was no inviting, or for that matter, uninviting, place to sit. Except for two pay phones on the wall, the sterile blankness was unbroken, and the room chilled me even though it was full of people. I overheard as many snippets of conversation about the murder and scene of the crime as I did about the cast and play.

Arturo and Amy enjoyed the spotlight, Amy seeing it as a guarantee of UCB. I had to remain aloof so as not to let my sour mood dampen her glee. While attending a certain school might open a few doors, by the time Amy was my age, no one would give a shit where she'd gone to college.

I felt glum because the recognition had come to me at a steep price. Publicly, to avoid looking like curmudgeons, the school's administration and the police gave the three of us reserved praise. Privately, they were very displeased. They didn't like that a civilian had become so entangled in their case. Clearly the outcome could have been quite different. Now not only the Santa Cruz Police Department, but also the Watsonville Police Department considered me a pain in the ass. How would I ever be able to transition into a career as a P.I.?

In the meantime, I was stuck in my job as a baker with a miffed boss. Eldon held me personally responsible for Alvina's suffering. She'd never forgive herself for mixing the cookie dough matter into a volatile bomb that had blown the lid off the school. Some colleagues, like the drama teacher Becky Rivas, went out of their way to befriend Alvina, but others, like Viola Goicovich, treated Alvina with open hostility.

"This school is over a hundred years old," Alvina told Eldon, "and there's never been a bigger rift between faculty."

Eldon conveyed this information to me with unstrained displeasure.

Twenty-five years of good-old-boy mentality died hard, I guess. Not everyone was glad to have Ed Smith revealed as the killer. Even in the enlightened world of educators, some thought Jennifer had "deserved it." She'd manipulated Ed Smith to get her pregnant, to avoid costly, unreliable inseminations, and then she'd blackmailed him, milking two incomes rather than one from her pregnancy. Yale was expensive.

These particular school employees didn't see that Ed Smith could only be used because he already had a proclivity in that direction. They didn't see a cancer had been cut away, only that a piece of their old life was missing.

I'd come to this performance for the kids, and because Becky Rivas had given me two tickets. But I hadn't been able to drag Chad to Watsonville. A month had passed and he still begrudged my involvement in the murder case.

"Ever hear of lying by omission," he'd asked, lighting a cigarette in my face. He'd rubbed salt in the wounds by taking his mom for Chinese food this very evening.

Chendo was singing to Arturo, or rather Joe Cable was singing to Emile that you've got to be taught to hate. I'd never told Alvina that Chendo put betel nut in the cookie dough, leaving him room to confess to her.

For a moment I quieted myself. Playing Joe Cable, Chendo could let his sensitivity and vulnerability show. He didn't have Arturo's voice or Jennifer's commanding presence, but his delicate tenor conveyed a depth of feeling. My appreciation for the students on the stage, for their perseverance and grappling with life, extended to the unknown figures in the near-capacity crowd.

Chendo made an endearing Joe Cable. He danced in front of the phony volcano, and suddenly Ed Smith clamped my arms behind me, twisting them. Lava boiled from my gut to my chest. I could've killed him. I hated him for destroying Jennifer. I hated him for humiliating me.

Did we have to be taught to hate? Like stereotypes, the lyrics of Chendo's song were true and untrue, just as the play was both a fact and fiction. The eruption of hatred in me hadn't required any teaching. It had been a natural, primal emotion.

In the dark of the auditorium, my thoughts turned inward, my stereotypes and prejudices melted away. I breathed deeply, releasing some of my anger toward Ed Smith. Some of it was frustration at my own life. I needed to make changes, to seek my Bali Hai, my own special island where my dreams could come true.

The play beckoned me toward the magical place of my future.

###

Thank you for reading my book. If you enjoyed One Tough Cookie, please look for the other books in the Carol Sabala series. If you write a review and contact me, I will send you your next Carol Sabala novel for free.

ACKNOWLEDGMENTS

I owe thanks to many people: my mother Vivian Hansen and my husband Daniel Friedman, who have been fabulous promoters of my first book. A special thanks goes to Herb Jellinek for his proofreading and his computer assistance. Kimiye Welch, Justin Owens, and Christine Kopecky all kindly read the manuscript in its embryonic stage. And of course, thanks to the ladies at misterio press!

ABOUT THE AUTHOR

Vinnie Hansen fled the South Dakota prairie for the California coast the day after graduating high school.

Author of the Carol Sabala mysteries, Vinnie was a Claymore Award finalist for *Black Beans & Venom,* the seventh installment in her series (misterio press). She's also written many published short stories including *Novel Solution,* in the anthology *Fish or Cut Bait* (Wildside Press).

Retired after 27 years of teaching English at Watsonville High School, Vinnie lives in Santa Cruz with her husband, abstract artist Daniel S. Friedman. Discover more at www.vinniehansen.com.

VINNIEHANSEN.COM

RECIPE FOR CRINKLES

This recipe came to me from Anne Stagnaro, one of the famous Santa Cruz Stagnaro clan. She and I were members of the same reading group, Women of Mystery. She often baked these crinkles for us before she passed away in 2009 at age 93. I've modified the recipe to fit my food politics.

½ cup veg. oil (non GMO)
4 squares (4 ounces) unsweetened chocolate, melted (fair traded and organic)
2 cups granulated sugar (organic)
4 eggs (local and cage-free)
2 tsp. vanilla (Rain's)
2 cups flour (organic)
2 tsp. baking powder
½ tsp salt (I seldom add this salt.)
powdered sugar (organic)
¾ cup of California walnuts

Mix well the oil, chocolate and sugar
Blend in one egg at a time
Add vanilla
Stir in flour, baking powder and salt (a little at a time works best)
Blend well and refrigerate over night
Next day: roll into balls (about the size of a Ping-Pong ball) and cover with confectionary sugar. Place two inches apart on cookie sheet and bake for 10 – 12 minutes. I like my cookies thoroughly baked (crispy not chewy), so it's always closer to 12 minutes for me, and sometimes I still add a bit more time.

Tip: Between batches, return the remaining dough to the refrigerator.

Makes between 3 and 4 dozen cookies, depending on size.

www.ingramcontent.com/pod-product-compliance
Lightning Source LLC
Chambersburg PA
CBHW072133170626
46813CB00004BA/1552